KAWATINA

roadwalker
PUBLISHING

KAWATINA

Byron Christensen

OTHER BOOKS BY THE AUTHOR

THREE

The Gratombe

The sun slid down the far side of the hill. Watina sat at the edge of the riverbank. Her mother, Kawutinee, picked berries across the river. She watched Watina through thick bushes. She knew she was different. She had outgrown playing with the other young girls. She learned how to do things quickly. She knew how to catch large pike from a deep hole in the river. She shot grouse with a bow her father had given her.

There had been challenging winters when it had been difficult to hunt moose in the deep snow. When rabbit snares were empty. Watina's father could do little to help gather food after having fallen through river ice many years earlier, a broken leg having set awkwardly.

Summer had been good. Many fish had been dried. Smoked moose meat and many baskets of dried berries were covered under heavy moss. Winter would be long and cold, Watina had told her mother. There was still need to get meat. There was always need for meat.

There were nights when Watina had dreamed of great fires burning. In the mornings, sitting behind their fire at the top of the hill, they would talk about them. As the dreams persisted Watina thought she might see something in their own fire from the riverbank far below.

A cloudy moon blurred the darkness as they sat at the fire one night. After Kawutinee had fallen asleep Watina slipped down the steep path to the river. It was early morning when Kawutinee was awakened by the sound of screaming. Calling, she waded into the dark river. Watina lay in the rippling water, her small, thin leg wedged between submerged logs. Crying her name, Kawutinee freed her and carried her lifeless body across the river. She buried her there.

1

A flock of pigeons circled the roof of a grain elevator at the end of a somber Sunday street. A scraggy dog slipped into an alley behind a narrow hardware store.

Gobs of rain slid down a café window. Leonard shifted in his seat. It was ten o'clock. Dayton was late. He was like that. He did things on his own time. At his convenience. He had phoned earlier. He was looking to buy a used tire because there was a slow leak in the back tire of his truck and he wasn't in the mood to buy a new one. Leonard lit a hand-rolled cigarette. The waitress came with more coffee. "Waiting can be a real pain sometimes, can't it?" She went to the window and looked down the street. "Dayton's parking his truck now." She went back to the kitchen when he arrived.

"I thought ya must have got lost," Leonard said.

"I had to stop in at the apartment to make sure the new janitor had the keys."

"All my stuff's sitting in the corner o' the shop. We can pick up a few groceries on the way out."

"It said on the radio that it's supposed to rain all week."

"It could make for some good fishin'. All we need is your stuff and we're ready to go."

"How long is it going to take to get there?"

"Five hours. Five or six hours."

"I don't even have a raincoat."

"That's what I forgot. My raincoat. Be right back."

A dimly-lit suite above an automotive garage smelled of burned bacon. Faded green wallpaper covered the walls. A stack of books rested on an old butter box beside a plain bed. A trouble light hung from a nail in the ceiling directly above it. Leonard rummaged through a cardboard box in a corner of the room.

Digging out a raincoat, he rolled it up and stuffed it under his arm.

Dayton was waiting in his truck when he got back down to the street. "I didn't know you had toast," he said. "I was going to pay for your coffee but she said you had toast with it."

Leonard ran in the rain back to the café. "I didn't mean to run off on ya like that without payin'."

"Put your money back in your pocket, Leonard. I'll get it this time. When you get back from your fishing trip you can take me to the mini-golf like you've been promising for months."

Leonard dropped change into a newspaper machine, grabbed a paper and jumped into Dayton's truck. "We can be out o' here in half an hour."

2

Whispers of wind crept over the hilltop. A small fire crackled. Slivers of poplar peeled away as a small knife worked soft, green wood.

Allan leaned against a boulder. Trees over a hundred years old stood below him. He spat on a whetstone.

This was the best place. No one ever came here. It was quiet and free. You could think about things without having to worry about what other people thought. You could do what you wanted without getting in anybody's way because nobody else was around.

That was why he came here. There was no one around to say anything or get in his way. He could carve and think without having to worry about other people. Sometimes he wished there weren't any other people around at all.

Only him.

3

By late afternoon the rolling prairie was several hundred miles behind them. The highway crept through thick boreal forests and fire-burned hillsides.

"I think you should pull into that gas station up the road," Leonard said. "I've been smellin' fumes. I think ya might have a leak in your gas tank."

Dayton parked the truck a short distance from the gas pumps. Leonard pulled his long, greying hair behind his ears and climbed out. Two elderly native men sitting on plastic chairs in the shade of a detached automotive garage watched as the travelers entered the gas station.

It was an older building that smelled of fresh bread, coffee and mysterious garage smells. A short balding man, unpacking potato chips at the end of a coffee counter, looked up. "How are you today?"

"Real good. You wouldn't have any gas tank sealant kicking around by any chance?"

"I think I've got something like that up here somewhere." He looked along an assortment of shelves. "By golly, I thought I had some of that stuff."

"No sweat," Leonard said. "I'll rub it down with soap for now. Is there an air pump outside someplace?"

"Around the corner of the garage. I'll have to turn it on." They went outside.

"My name's Chap. I run this outfit. It looks like you're going to do a little canoeing."

"I'm Leonard, and this good-lookin' young man is Dayton. We thought we'd get out to one o' the lakes around here and do a little fishin'."

Chap ran his hand along the rough, blistered skin of a wood and canvas canoe strapped in the back of the truck. "Where are you headed today?"

"According to our topographical map there's an abandoned road north o' here somewhere. We thought we'd follow it in for a ways and set up camp back in the bush. We're gonna hike over to the river and try our luck there for a day or two before we take the canoe out."

"You picked a good time to come up. It's been raining for weeks but the sun's been shining the past few days. If it stays like this you should have some nice fishing weather. There's a road crew working a few miles north of here. The abandoned road you're talking about is only a mile or so south of their camp."

"I don't think we'll have any trouble findin' it. I've been studyin' the map and it looks like it's on the south side of a small hill."

"It might be a little tough to find. It's grown over pretty thick with willows by now. You might have to do a little walking. And you might want to be careful driving along the stretch of road near the hill. We've had quite a few accidents in that area." Chap turned and headed back to the gas station. "Stop in sometime and let me know how you made out with your fishing. I've always got the coffee pot on."

Leonard filled the tire. In fifteen minutes they reached the crest of a small hill. Below them, a short distance away, an assortment of heavy road construction equipment was clustered in a large clearing at the edge of the highway.

They pulled over and climbed out. Leonard laid the map across the hood of the truck. "According to this it looks like the abandoned road should be a mile or so south o' here."

Dayton turned the truck around and drove along the edge of the highway, stopping a few minutes later at an overgrown trail barely visible for the second growth covering it. "I'm not going to take the truck in there. It's going to get scratched."

"I don't think a few more scratches on this old thing are gonna make much difference."

It was slow going. Willows lashed the windows. Holes of questionable depth were filled with water. Dayton stopped the truck and pulled at a branch snagged in the side view mirror. By early evening a large canvas wall tent had been roped up between two trees. A large fire was burning. Leonard pulled a blackened wiener off a willow stick and wrapped a slice of bread around it. Dunking it into his coffee, he shoved half of it into his mouth. Dayton, sitting against a tree, pulled his cap over his eyes.

"This is a great campin' spot, man. I don't think we'll have to worry about anybody botherin' us around here."

Dayton's eyes were closed, his mouth open. He had complained about getting the truck scratched. He had wanted to turn back and go somewhere else. He pouted a lot. When he was tired he pouted more.

Leonard grabbed the axe and started walking down the trail they had come in on toward the highway, a quarter of a mile away.

"Where are you going?" Dayton muttered.

"I'm gonna clean out some o' the second growth on the trail."

"I'm going to have a nap." Dayton pulled a thick sleeping bag out of the tent and laid it in front of the fire.

"If I'm not back by sunset you'll know I cut my leg off and bled to death."

It was growing dark when he returned to camp. His arms were scratched. A blotch of blood soaked through the back of his shirt. "There's a lot o' willow out there, but at least now we can see where we're goin'." He pulled a large plastic pail out of the box of the truck. "How's the coffee?"

"I just woke up a few minutes ago. Look at this." Dayton stroked a large burn hole in his sleeping bag.

"Nothin' a little duct tape can't fix. We'll pick some up next time we're at the gas station." Leonard filled the coffee pot with water from a plastic water canister and dug two cans of stew out of a wooden box in the back of the truck. Gathering a handful of small, dry branches, he shoved them into the fire and blew into the coals. "If we get an early start in the mornin' we'll make good time gettin' to the river."

4

They came upon a large beaver dam after a couple of hour's hiking. It didn't take long before they started catching fish.

Leonard walked the length of a partially-submerged log. His line was caught up on a submerged log thirty feet out.

"You're going to end up falling in if you're not careful. Losing hooks is part of fishing, Leonard. Just break the line and forget about it."

"I've caught four fish with this hook and I don't have another one like it." After unsuccessfully trying to dislodge the hook, he wrapped the line around his hand and pulled it tight until it snapped. "How much farther do you think it is to the river?"

"Probably a couple of miles."

"Things are lookin' good, if ya ask me. Whoever built the campsite here did a heck of a job. We've got a big tarpaulin lean-to, a homemade fuel drum stove, a shovel, a bucksaw, a hatchet and a spring-fed creek a stone's throw away." He pulled out his tobacco and sprinkled it onto a thin leaf of cigarette paper. "Do ya want to head to the river after we have a bite to eat or would ya rather stay here?"

Dayton pulled at the tab of a pop can, took a long drink and belched. "After I eat I think I'm going to relax."

"I'm a little stiff, myself. We may as well stay here tonight. I'm gonna hike up to the top o' this ridge behind us after we eat. It looks like it'll be the best way to get around the muskeg along the edge of the beaver pond. I wouldn't mind climbin' that hill over yonder, either. It must be a heck of a view from up there."

***** ***** *****

Leonard sat under the gaping boughs of a large spruce tree. Fog hugged the riverbank.

Dayton was still at the beaver pond. He liked it there. It was comfortable, and he could sleep.

Unlashing the axe from his packboard, Leonard walked back into the bush to gather firewood. Crouching in a splatter of brown-eyed Susans, he rolled a cigarette. A grouse feather fluttered in the long grass. Plucking it and sticking it into his shirt pocket, he leaned against a moss-covered log and rolled a cigarette.

Dayton was sprawled out on his sleeping bag when Leonard got back to the river. He pulled on Dayton's boot.

"I was trying to have a nap," Dayton grunted, "but there's too many bugs. Where have you been?"

"Just walkin' around. I think I might have seen some bear tracks, but it's hard to say."

"I should of brought my rifle!"

"I'm gonna have a bite to eat and see if I can find a shallow spot in the river somewhere around here so we can wade across. I want to climb that hill."

Dayton looked up at the crest of a hill directly across the river from them. "It's more like a cliff."

"I thought it would be as good a place as any to spend the night."

"I better get something to eat, then." Dayton dug a package of doughnuts out of his pack.

"I'm gonna walk around for awhile."

*****   *****   *****

A cool breeze wafted a smoky fire. Dayton sat against a large boulder. Leonard, sitting against a boulder across from him, pulled out his tobacco pouch, turned his back to the breeze and rolled a cigarette. "This is really something. Can you imagine wrestlin' these boulders up here? They're bigger than a doghouse. I had enough trouble just walkin' up here. That must have been quite a job."

"Who would waste their time bringing a bunch of rocks all the way up here?"

"Must be campers or berry-pickers."

"I doubt that berry pickers would waste their time with a bunch of rocks."

"I'm talkin' about the firewood piled up here. Must be people comin' out from the city on weekends. I think the boulders have been here quite a while. I think Indians might have put 'em here back in the day."

"Oh yeah – like you're going to see a bunch of Indians with boulders on their backs climbing up this huge hill and building a fire so they can have a picnic." Dayton had a way of poisoning conversations when he wasn't interested in the topic.

"When we were across the river I didn't see bear tracks like I was tellin' ya, but I found something when I went for firewood. When you were still back at the beaver pond, when I was waitin' for ya."

"What are you talking about?"

"I found a couple o' rocks. They look the same as these boulders."

"This country's full of rocks. That's about all it's good for. Trees and rocks. And muskeg."

"When I told ya I was gonna walk around a bit I went back to where I was pokin' around for firewood. That was where I found the rocks. They have grooves in 'em, like these boulders."

"They probably got scratched up when a tree fell on them. I wish you would of told me the truth to begin with. I thought there was a bear around here."

"I didn't know for sure what the rocks were. That's why I went back with the axe."

"Somebody must of put them here, but I could care less."

"When we stopped at the gas station to get some glop to put on the gas tank – when

Chap turned on the air pump – there were two old native fellas sittin' in the shade beside the air hose. Chap asked me where we were headed and I pointed in this direction. I heard one o' the old boys say something when I pointed over here. When we pulled out onto the highway they were both standin' up, watching us. I'm thinkin' they might know something about the boulders. I'd be interested in talking to 'em."

"How are you going to do that? Smoke signals?"

"I'd like to borrow your truck and go back to the gas station."

"They're not going to be there now. They were probably waiting to catch the bus."

"The guy who owns the gas station might know 'em. Or he might know where I can find 'em."

"We came up here to do some fishing, and that's what I'm going to do. I could care less about a bunch of boulders. I'll go back with you as far as the beaver pond, but that's as far as I'm going."

"I'll show ya where I found the rocks when we cross the river."

5

Leonard pulled into the gas station and slouched onto one of the stools along a coffee counter. Chap emerged from a back room. "Hello there. How's the fishing?"

"Real good."

"Are you hungry? How about some ham and eggs?"

"Sounds good. I've got a question for ya. When we stopped here the other day there were a couple of native fellas sittin' outside. Older fellas."

"They come in every now and again to pick up a few things."

"Any idea where they'd be now?"

"They camp at a lake not far from here."

"I'm thinkin' they might know a bit about this country."

"They've been in this area as long as I can remember. They're getting up in years now but they don't speak English. When they buy something I put it on a tab and a younger fella who's with them quite a bit pays the bill. There's another younger fella who camps with them but he never says much. They're at the lake every summer, 'til the snow flies. I have an idea they're from the Slave Lake area. The younger fellas were here the other day and picked them up. The same day you were here."

"What kind o' truck were they drivin'?"

"It's an orange-red Ford pickup."

"Do you think the old boys would be at the lake today?"

"It's hard to say. They come and go. They drive an older truck and I think they might be having a little trouble with it. That might be why the other two fellas picked them up the other day. One of the local pipeline inspectors drops in now and then to shoot the breeze, and he mentioned seeing an old green Chevy half ton parked by the side of the road a few miles from here. I know that's the truck the old fellas drive when they come here for gas and propane. Whether they'd be at the lake or not is hard to say."

"How far is it to the lake?"

"Twenty miles, give or take."

"What kind o' shape is the road in?"

"It's pretty greasy with the rain we've been getting all summer. And it's going to start raining again by the looks of things."

"Is the road marked?"

"Someone slid into the sign and knocked it over last winter. But the turnoff's only a few miles north of here. It's about an hour's drive to the lake, maybe a bit more."

*****   *****   *****

A narrow gravel road plunged through large stands of spruce and skirted thick, dank stretches of muskeg. Gobs of rain smattered the windshield A tanker truck heading toward him pounded through water-filled holes. Leonard grasped the steering wheel with both hands and pulled over. A tide of mud water drenched the truck. Over the course of an hour a dozen trucks passed, moving an oil rig out of the bush. Leonard filled the windshield washer reservoir with ditch water and wrestled the truck back onto the road, scarred with ruts deep enough to bury a power pole.

It was another hour before he reached a small lake. A canvas wall tent sat at the far end of a logged-out clearing along the lake's edge. A small aluminum boat, haltered to a post, waltzed in the water on a rocky shoreline.

Leonard tightened the collar of his denim jacket and slogged a hundred yards to the campsite. A tarpaulin covered a pile of split firewood. An axe protruded from a splitting log. A rusty bow saw dangled from a tree branch.

"Hello! Anybody home?" Leonard shouted against the wind. He went inside the tent. A cot rested on either side of a small airtight stove. A thick down-filled sleeping bag had been stuffed under one of them.

He pulled a plastic pail out from under a small wooden table, sat down and rolled a cigarette. A thin jackknife rested beside a small carving on the table. Four coffee cups – two from a trucking outfit, one from a restaurant, the other a brown clay cup with a lashed willow handle – sat in a waterless basin on the stove. A few candles, a roll of paper towels stuffed into a bread wrapper and an old camera hung from a plastic bag in the corner.

Wind whipped the tent. Butting the cigarette in his pant cuff, he replaced the plastic pail, crawled out of the tent and with the wind whipping his face ran back to the truck. It had been a long hike from the river back to their main camp. He was tired and hungry. He started the truck, spread peanut butter on two slices of bread and wolfed them down. Fashioning a pillow from a raincoat, he pulled a blanket out from behind the seat and fell asleep.

Early morning awakened him with a rush of birdcalls. The rain had stopped. Jagged rays of sunlight spoked thick clouds. Pulling on his wet boots, he slopped to the lake edge and walked the shoreline for an hour.

A warm breeze rippled the water when he headed back to the camp. When he reached the edge of the clearing he noticed two men standing at his truck. One of them, a lean native with a long braided ponytail, noticed him and approached. The other man, younger, clutching a tire iron, watched. The two elderly men he had previously seen at the gas station unloaded groceries from the back of a red pickup.

A boney hand was offered him. "My name's Nestor. You have a low tire."

"I'm Leonard. Looks like I'm gonna have to get that patched."

"We were going to put the spare tire on and had the truck jacked up halfway before we realized you don't have one. There's a hand pump in the tent we use for the air mattress. That should get you rolling again. I think we pushed our truck halfway here. They moved a big rig out yesterday and the road's torn up quite a bit."

"I got caught in the middle of it."

They approached the younger man.

"Allan," Nestor said, "this is Leonard."

Allan nodded.

"Leonard says there's a slow leak in the tire." Allan went to the tent.

Leonard rolled a smoke. "I was in your tent for a while. I wanted to see if anyone was home."

Allan returned with the air pump and began tightening the lug nuts on the tire.

"Would you like some coffee?" Nestor said.

"Sounds good. I'll pump up the tire first."

"I can do it," Allan said.

Nestor and Leonard headed toward the tent. "Allan doesn't talk much. He's pretty quiet around strangers."

The old boys were sitting on the cots. One of them, wearing a thick green flannel shirt, picked at his thumbnail. The other, holding the willow branch-handled coffee cup to his chest, looked up at Leonard and grinned.

Leonard squatted under the tent flap and pulled the cigarette out of his shirt pocket.

Nestor poured coffee. "We drink it black."

"I do, too."

"The owner of the gas station said someone wanted to talk to us about something."

"That was me. My buddy and I came up to do a little fishin'. We hiked over to the river and I found a couple o' rocks that had some interesting markings on 'em. They were the same kind o' markings that are on some boulders up on a big hill across the river. I'm thinkin' the rocks and the boulders on the hill have something in common."

Allan came in. "What did you do with them?"

"I left 'em there. I was gatherin' firewood and sat down to have a smoke. That's how I found 'em. I wanted to spend the night up on the hill so I could check out the view. When we got to the top there was a fire pit and three boulders that had the same kind o' markings on 'em that the rocks had."

"Excuse us for a minute," Nestor said. "We'll be right back."

Nestor and Allan went outside. Inaudible murmurings soaked through the thick canvas tent. Nestor returned in a few minutes.

"Allan has a lean-to near the hill he goes to now and then. Did you see it?"

"There's a tarpaulin lean-to at a beaver pond east o' the river, if that's the one ya mean. We spent the night there when we were headed for the river."

"That isn't it," Nestor said. "Allan's lean-to is north of the hill, on the east side of the river."

"I didn't do too much walkin' around."

"The hill is the highest one in the country. It has a lot of significance to us."

"I kind o' figured that after I saw that the rocks I found near the river had the same kind o' markings on 'em as the boulders on the hill. That's why I was hopin' I could catch up with the old fellas. I'd like to ask 'em a few questions. Just out o' curiosity. But they don't speak English, according to what Chap said. He told me there's a new road goin' in someplace but we didn't see anything that looked like a road where we were."

"We're not sure what they're doing. We think they might be putting in a new oil rig west of the highway somewhere."

"Any chance you guys will be goin' out to the hill sometime soon?"

"We go out now and then but when it rains like this we usually stay here. The pickup's just a two wheel drive."

"Might you be interested in goin' out with me and Dayton?"

"There aren't many people who go that far back." Nestor dug a piece of paper out of the tinderbox. Pulling a pencil stub from his shirt pocket he printed something on the paper and handed it to Leonard.

"Kawa..."

"Kawatina," Nestor said. "The accent is on the second syllable. Ka WAT in a."

"Ka WAT in a," Leonard repeated.

"The hill and the area around it is Kawatina," Nestor said.

"If you're not up to goin' out there I don't have a problem with that. Maybe we'll see you guys out there sometime." Leonard pulled open the tent flap to leave.

"Give us a few minutes," Nestor said.

Leonard strolled to the edge of the water and sat on a rock. Several minutes later Nestor and Allan joined him.

"We can go out with you tomorrow," Nestor said. "Allan has a few things he wants to take out to his lean-to."

"There's a big beaver pond I was tellin' ya about a mile or so east of the hill. Somebody's got a camp set up there."

"Hunters."

"That's where my fishin' buddy is. He's not too big on doin' any extra walking so he said he was going to stay there 'til I got back."

They talked into the night.

At daybreak they headed out. By mid afternoon they reached the beaver pond.

Dayton stood up as the trio approached.

"I'd like you to meet a couple o' friends o' mine," Leonard said. "This is Nestor." He swung around. "And this is Allan."

Leonard went to the spring and filled his cupped hands with water. Nestor and Allan joined him. "I helped myself to a couple o' cans o' your fruit cocktail back in camp," Leonard said.

"I only brought six cans out with me."

"Next trip into town I'll pick up some." Leonard opened them with his knife and dumped the contents into four coffee cups. Shoveling the fruit down, he leaned back. "How about I catch half a dozen trout and we'll cook 'em up."

"There's five on the stringer," Dayton said.

"Right on. We'll get a fire goin' and I'll gut 'em."

"I'll build the fire," Nestor said. Allan went into the bush to gather wood.

Nestor talked sporadically while they ate. Allan sat off to the side but said nothing. Taking off his boots, Leonard stretched out on thick moss and rolled a cigarette. Heavy thunder rolled in the distance.

"The rocks Leonard found near the river are headstones," Nestor said to Dayton. "There are two graves there."

Allan went to the edge of the pond. Nestor joined him. Allan stuffed a large gob of snuff under his lip. Returning to the fire, he hoisted his packsack and walked toward the ridge, disappearing into the trees.

"Looks like he isn't happy," Leonard said

"He doesn't like being around other people very much. We'll catch up to him at the hill."

"How old is he?"

"Twenty seven."

Leonard scratched his stubbled face and looked toward the ridge. "Let's get our things together and get out o' here."

6

Nestor stood beside a large fire on top of the hill and pointed north.

"A girl was born not far from here. Her name was Watina. Her mother's name was Kawutinee. When Watina was a young girl Kawutinee brought her here to fish in the river. In the afternoon when the sun dropped behind the hill it created a shadow across the river. Watina learned that the fish would move into the shadow of the hill to get into the cooler water. Kawutinee showed her how to set snares for rabbits and squirrels. They were the first ones to camp on the hill. They built the first fire here. When Watina grew older she talked about dreams she often had of fires burning up the land. One day she drowned in the river. Kawutinee carried her to the other side. That was where she buried her. It was a hard winter that year. Kawutinee also died. She was buried beside her daughter. The graves you found were theirs."

Leonard studied the thick of green below him. "This is where they used to hang out, so to speak."

"This was Watina's favourite place. The others didn't come this far but Watina and her mother spent many summers here."

"There could be a hundred graves down there, for all we know."

"When you came here to do a little fishing you ended up in an area that at one time had a great deal of spiritual significance to our people. But over the years they began moving farther away, and it became too difficult to bring family members back for a ceremonial burial. Many graves are 'lost' because when our people moved on they left no word about their family members' whereabouts."

"The new road they're puttin' in. Do you have any idea if it's gonna come over this far?"

"It's hard to say," Nestor said, "but the muskeg on the west side of the beaver pond gets wider as you go north. If that's where they plan on putting the road I don't think they'll get through."

"How long has the road crew been here?"

"Not very long, but I can't say for sure."

"Maybe we should tell 'em about the graves," Leonard said.

"I came here to fish," Dayton spouted. "Not talk about graves."

"What about Forestry?" Leonard said. "They must know about 'em."

"Nobody knows about them," Allan said. "Just us."

"It might be a good idea to let the road guys know about the graves. To be on the safe side."

Allan stood up and reached for his packsack. Nestor walked away from the fire and motioned for Allan to join him. They spoke in Cree. Allan headed toward a narrow trail leading down the hill and disappeared.

Nestor came back to the fire. "I'm going to spend the night with Allan at his lean-to. If you want to get an idea of what the muskeg looks like you can meet up with us in the morning. We'll be at a long bend in the river a mile north of here. We can hike back to the highway from there, across the muskeg. We might be able to see where they've got the road staked out."

*   *   *

A smudged moon hung in the early evening. Leonard rolled three large logs onto the fire.

"Why is the fire so big?"

"I'm gonna take off for a while. Keep it burnin' as high as ya can."

"Where are you going?"

"Down to the gravesite."

"I can think of better ways of spending the night than going all the way down there, freezing my balls off crossing the river. It's going to be getting dark pretty soon."

"I've got a flashlight. There's plenty o' wood here. Keep it burning as high as ya can."

When he reached the opposite bank of the river he went to the gravesite where he had found the marked rocks. The hill was concealed behind thick bush. Back at the riverbank, he smoked cigarettes and listened to the river. As darkness thickened, the hilltop fire glowed above him.

By the time he returned to the crest of the hill it was pitch dark. Dayton was leaning against a boulder.   An empty cake box lay beside him.

"Havin' a little party, are we?"

"I figured that if we were going to be roughing it for a few weeks I'd make myself as comfortable as I could, so I brought a cake. I was going to save some for you but I thought that by the time you got back it would be dried out."

Leonard filled a mug with cold coffee and set the pot back in the fire. "Ya gotta love it out here. It beats the heck out o' smelling gas fumes all day."

"How long have you been working at the garage?" Dayton said.

"A little better than a year."

"Where are you from?"

"Ontario. Six Nations."

"Is that where your family is?"

"I have an older brother. But he took off when I was sixteen. I haven't seen him since."

"Are your parents still there?"

Leonard waited before he spoke. "They were killed in a car accident." He paused again. "It was tough, losin' 'em. We were pretty close. And we had a pretty good life. The old man was a trucker. He worked hard and treated us all as well as could be expected from someone who's away most o' the time. I had a bit o' trouble concentratin' on things after they died. My brother and the old man were pretty close. He wanted to learn how to drive a semi so he could spend more time with him. It was only a couple o' weeks or so after the accident when he took off. He didn't come home one night and I haven't seen him since."

Leonard rolled a smoke and fired it up. "I may as well give ya my life story in a nutshell while I'm in the mood. It might help you understand why I do some o' the things I do. I ended up droppin' out o' school. I kicked around for a couple o' years, workin' wherever I could get a job, and ended up in a furniture factory. I was always pretty good with machinery. I ended up bein' the head forklift operator. It took a while to get used to the night shift but we got paid a little more than the day shift and after a couple o' months I could sleep through dogs barkin' and horns honkin' all day. The bunch I worked with was pretty good. I ended up stayin' there for several years.

"I met a gal at the laundromat one morning and we started hangin' out a bit. I asked her to marry me four months later. She turned out to be the best thing that ever happened to me. We bought a house and had a little girl. Her name was Lyla. She was so much like her mother. She was my pride 'n joy.

"She was comin' home from school one day and ran across the street in front of a car that had stopped to let her cross. Somebody who was in a hurry passed the car that was stopped...and she ended up on the other side o' the road. She was in Intensive Care for a couple o' weeks...but she was crumpled up pretty bad. I worked like a dog at the furniture plant to keep my mind off o' things. I didn't realize it at the time but I was paying more attention to myself than tryin' to help my wife get through it. I got home one morning and the bedroom door was closed. She had left me a note on the kitchen table. She was wearin' the pantsuit she was gonna wear on our holidays.

"I buried her beside our daughter and everything pretty well went for shit after that. I sold the house and learned how to ride a motorcycle. I spent the next couple o' years or so flyin' down every road in the country. About the only thing I owned was a sleeping bag and a pup tent. I didn't give a damn about anybody, includin' myself. One morning I woke up on the floor of a SallyAnn crashpad in Edmonton. To this day I don't know how I got there, but I was sicker than a dog. And my bike was gone. One o' the councillors at the

SallyAnn was a Slavee Indian. He told me he moved down to Edmonton from the Territories a couple o' years earlier so he could sell his stone carvings. Someone told him that the guy he was selling 'em to in the Territories was rippin' him off and selling 'em for a small fortune in the city.

"He thought the best thing to do would be to go to Edmonton and sell them himself. But when he got to the city he didn't know anybody. After a few weeks passed and he only sold two carvings he realized there weren't a hell of a lot o' people out on the sidewalk who were interested in buyin' his stuff. He got caught up in the booze a little, and then a little became a lot. One day someone pulled him out from under a sheet o' cardboard on the outskirts of town somewhere and brought him to the SallyAnn. He was there for a long time and ended up kind o' working there.

"We got to know each other pretty good while I was there and agreed to keep in touch. I stuck around the Edmonton area because I could always find work there without havin' to go too far. About six months later I fell off the wagon. I wanted to get in touch with my new friend so I went to the SallyAnn to track him down. They told me he had jumped off the

High Level Bridge a couple o' weeks earlier. That was a little tough to take because I was under the impression he was on Sober Street. I started walking a little bit, to try and get a clearer view of things, and tried to eat at least one good meal a day."

"At least you recognized what the problem was."

"I did. But it was tough goin'. Like any good alcoholic I always had a pocketful of excuses at the ready to defend myself when necessary. It's easier to blame an addiction on somebody else than to face the music and admit you brought it on yourself. My argument with Alcoholics Anonymous is that the writers of the books AA members are encouraged to read make the assertion alcoholism is a disease. But that couldn't be farther from the truth. Alcoholism is an addiction. It's not some kind of incurable disease AA members are led to believe it is. Thousands of people have quit drinkin'. The road to sobriety can be tough, but like anything else in life you get out of it what you put into it. I'm getting carried away with this so I better stop talkin'."

7

Drizzle thickened the morning air. Nestor sat at a small fire. Leonard approached.

"Good morning, Leonard."

"Mornin'." Leonard took a cup of coffee handed him. Dayton dropped his packsack to the ground and sat against a tree, away from the fire.

"It looks like you fell in the river," Nestor said.

"I didn't bother takin' off my pants when we crossed the river. They were still wet from last night, anyway."

"What were you doing in the river last night?" Nestor said.

"I was hopin' to see the fire on the hill from the gravesite, but there's too much bush."

"How did you sleep? It can get a little chilly up there if the wind's blowing."

"I feel pretty good, all things considered. Do you think the road will end up around here someplace?"

"The muskeg is behind us, just east of here. If they go due west from their camp, in the direction they're going now, they won't be able to get past it."

"Why don't we fill up on coffee and head toward the highway."

It was late afternoon by the time they had slogged across the muskeg. They had found and followed a narrow survey line, leading them to the new road on firm ground. They followed it to the construction camp. Ahead of them, a dirty white four wheel drive was parked at the south end of the camp clearing. Two men, leaning against the truck, saw them and approached. One, dressed in greasy coveralls, spoke.

"This road easement is private property."

"We're hikin' today," Leonard said. "We're camped just south o' here. We were wondering if the road is gonna keep goin' west along the survey line we followed across the muskeg."

The other man, clean cut, wearing a sports shirt and khaki pants, replied. "We're putting a new road in across the river into a timber berth." He adjusted his white hard hat.

"There's quite a bit o' muskeg back there we just slogged through. It starts where your survey markers are."

"I'm the foreman here," the coveralled man said. He lifted his cap and ran a dirty hand through greasy hair. "A little muskeg never bothered me."

"The road's goin' west o' here then, is it?"

The foreman peeled off his coveralls. "We're going across the river into a timber berth. We already told you that."

The man in khaki pants motioned to the foreman. They walked off a short distance. The man in khaki pants looked toward Allan, sitting off to the side, and laughed.

Allan picked up his packsack and started walking toward the highway. Nestor caught up with him and returned a few minutes later.

"What's up?" Leonard said.

"Allan doesn't like the khaki pants guy."

The foreman came over. "You better catch up to your friend. He might get lost."

"We have some information you might be interested in," Leonard said.

"You've told us about the muskeg we already know about. What else do you want to tell us that we already know?" He picked up his coveralls and jammed them under his armpit.

"Not now. Tomorrow, maybe."

KhakiPants stepped up. "How would it be if you drop by in the morning?" He pointed to a small white trailer at the far end of the camp clearing. "But you'll have to go directly to the office. There's a lot of big equipment rumbling around first thing in the morning and you don't want to get in anybody's way."

"That would be good," Nestor said.

"But not before eight o'clock."

KhakiPants and the foreman jumped into their truck and headed toward the office trailer.

"That foreman character thinks he's pretty slick, doesn't he?" Leonard said. They gathered their packsacks and headed toward the highway.

Allan stood, waiting. He and Nestor fell back and talked. When Leonard and Dayton reached camp they built a fire. Nestor joined them later, without Allan.

"Are you guys okay with seeing the roadboys in the mornin'?"

"I think we should wait," Nestor said. "Until we know where the road's going. Allan and I were talking about it. He thinks we should find out as much as we can about what their plans are. He doesn't want them to know about the graves."

"I can talk to 'em, if ya like. I'll tell 'em you've got a good hunting area over near the river someplace and that you're worried they might scare the game off with their equipment. You'd think that if they were already planning on detouring toward the hill, Slick there would have said something to that effect. I'll tell 'em you'd like to have an idea of where they plan on goin' so you can get a few days hunting in ahead o' the equipment."

Allan emerged from the trees and pulled a large tarpaulin from the back of their truck. He spread it on the ground and pulled one end over the opened tailgate. After having cut small pegs he pounded them into the tarpaulin holes, tightening the tarp as he made his way around. He untied his sleeping bag from his pack, rolled it into the temporary tent and crawled inside.

8

Thick fog shrouded the truck as Leonard descended the hill and pulled into the construction camp. He parked beside two trucks in front of the office trailer. The door opened when he reached the bottom of the steps.

"Hello there." KhakiPants, coffee cup in hand, motioned for him to come in. "It isn't the kind of weather a person wants to be out hiking in, is it? Grab yourself a coffee." The foreman, sitting at a small table, leafed through a stack of papers but said nothing. "Where are your partners this morning?" KhakiPants said. "I thought you were all coming in."

"There was a bit of an emergency last night," Leonard lied. "They had to run down to Whitecourt."

"I hope everything's all right." White teeth gleamed against KhakiPants' smooth, clean-shaven face. He went to the window. "They're calling for rain all week. It's tough to get a road built when it rains every day. So, you guys said you had something you wanted to talk about."

"We did, but the other guys aren't here so I thought I'd drop in to see how the road buildin' was coming."

"Not worth a damn," the foreman mumbled.

"We're having a go of it, that's for sure," KhakiPants said. "We can move a lot of dirt in a day when it's dry but with the weather we've been having I think I could dig as much with a tablespoon as we've moved with the equipment."

Leonard pointed to a large map taped to the wall above the table. "Is that map for this area?"

A thin red line had been penciled onto the map. "We're right…here," KhakiPants said, pulling a stir stick out of his mouth, using it as a pointer. "And once the rain stops and we can start getting some work done, we'll be right…here."

"Looks like you're basically going due west o' here. You don't think you'll have any trouble gettin' across the muskeg, then."

The foreman got up and refilled his coffee. "Where are you guys from?"

"Kroywen. Dayton and I are from Kroywen. Down in the badlands country. About twenty miles east o' Foxgull. Nestor and Allan are from the Slave Lake area."

"I thought you were brothers. The three of you, anyway. We have some paperwork to go over. Is there anything else?"

"I was just curious about where the road was goin'. Sounds like the other guys have a pretty good hunting area near the river somewhere and they were concerned the road might shake things up a bit."

"It doesn't matter what they're concerned about," the foreman chided. "*We're* here now. They'll have to hunt somewhere else."

KhakiPants went to the map. "Where, exactly, is this hunting ground of theirs?"

"You'll have to ask them."

"It's pretty hard to talk to somebody when they're not around," the foreman said.

He pulled a set of keys out of his pocket and went out to his truck.

"Don't pay any attention to him," KhakiPants said. "He's not the most congenial person at the best of times. I don't think your friends should have to worry about their hunting grounds. This is a big country. There's lots of game."

Leonard leaned on the table and peered at the map. "Yesterday we followed a narrow site-line runnin' basically east/west."

"That's our preliminary survey line."

"There's a pretty good stretch o' floatin' muskeg out there."

"We've got enough big dirt buggies to drag some fill in. It's all this rain we've been getting that's holding us back. It's frustrating as hell."

Leonard turned toward the door. "Just thought I'd drop in to see how things were goin'."

"I'm glad you did. What time did you say the other fellas would be getting back?"

"They didn't know. I better let you get back to your paperwork."

It was pouring when he pulled into camp. Nestor was crouched under the tarpaulin tailgate tent. Allan sat beside him at a small smoky fire, pushing his jackknife blade into a small whetstone.

"Mornin'."

"Good morning, Leonard," Nestor replied. "You were so quiet this morning I didn't hear anything until you started the truck. By the time I got out of the sleeping bag you were gone. How did you make out with the road boys?"

"I didn't learn much more than we already know. They've got some kind o' project map on the wall but they just penciled in where the road was. It didn't look very official. The site-line we followed is their preliminary survey line. According to what KhakiPants was saying they're gonna put fill across the muskeg."

"Some of that floating muskeg is bottomless. I think they're going to run into trouble if they try crossing it. I was going to mention something to you this morning but you got away on me."

Leonard filled a cup with cold coffee. "What's up?"

"There's a creek west of here. We crossed it coming back yesterday."

"Yup. I remember that."

"At one time it was a river. Before they built a dam upstream. Our people used it year 'round to get from camp to camp. It was their main thoroughfare through the bush. The generations before us knew the land west of the river was an area where there was always a lot of game. And lots of berries in the summer. Since they built the dam, what was once a river is now a shallow creek. It's a sign of the beginning of the end for the land west of the river, the way the old boys look at it. Oil companies have been doing a lot of exploration work in this area, and once they started developing their leases the game began to disappear. It bothers the old fellas to see the oil companies cut so many new lines through the bush. There might be a lot of oil in this area but there isn't much game anymore. And now they want to build a logging road that's going to go into an area that has some of the oldest trees in the country. It's one of the last pieces of virgin forest in the area. The old boys have seen a lot of changes over the years. They understand that the world around them is improving in many areas, but referring to it as 'progress' is a misnomer because in many cases the progress being referred to is destroying the earth."

"If I'm hearin' ya right you guys would just as soon see 'em stay out o' that area."

"We have the technology nowadays to build dams and highways and space shuttles and who knows what else, but that same technology is destroying the natural habitat. It's slowly but surely destroying the earth. We're losing sight of the fact that this can't go on forever. We're going to end up paying for it one way or another. Global warming is a good example. Look what's happening in the Arctic."

"I can't argue with that. I told 'em you guys couldn't make it this morning because you had to run down to Whitecourt. But we can see 'em now if ya like."

"Maybe now would be as good a time as any."

Leonard, Nestor and Allan piled into Nestor's truck. When they pulled into the roadcamp, Nestor spoke. "It seems to me that whether we like it or not, it would probably be best to tell them about the graves."

"Let's find out what they plan on doin' before we say anything," Leonard added.

They went to the office trailer. KhakiPants stood at the door, coffee cup in hand. "Come on in, fellas."

The foreman was sitting at the table, his hands clasped together. A heavy man with gunnysack jowls, wearing an expensive-looking suit, stood beside the filing cabinet.

Leonard pointed to the project map on the wall. "This is a forest cover map, isn't it?"

"Yes. It gives us a pretty good idea of where all the trees are out there," KhakiPants chortled.

Leonard pointed to the map. "Is this where you're going to put the road? North of the hill?"

The man in the suit craned his head around to look at the map beside him. "What hill are you talking about?"

"There's a hill west of here," Nestor said. "At the river. Do you have a topographical map?"

The foreman pulled a folded map out of the filing cabinet and spread it across on the table. "Where's this hill you're talking about?"

Leonard pointed. "Right here. On the west side o' the river."

"Okay, there you go. I see it," KhakiPants said. "What were you saying about this hill?"

"The road's going to be running pretty well due west of here according to the direction your survey line is headed."

"So what?" the foreman said.

"We don't have any concerns if it's going the direction it's been surveyed, but there are a couple o' things we think you should be made aware of. There are some important native interests around the hill, if it turns out that you have to move the road farther south in order to detour the muskeg."

"You mentioned that you're concerned about our scaring the game away with the equipment."

"That's just part of it."

The Suit peered at the wall map and the map on the table. "What exactly are these native interests?"

"There are two native graves out there."

"There's *what*?!"

"There are native graves east of the hill. On the east side of the river."

Khakipants pulled a toothpick out of his shirt pocket and pointed it at the hill. "You say there are two native graves out there."

Allan went to the table. He put his finger on the topographical map. "Right here."

"Hells Bells!" the foreman said. "The road isn't anywhere near there!"

"We're aware o' that," Leonard said. "As long as it's gonna go where you've got it staked out. But it's gonna be quite a chore to cross the floating muskeg west o' here. We know what we're talkin' about because we slogged through it. The only way we can see to get across the river and into your timber berth is to detour the road south, and cross the muskeg where it narrows down near the south end. But if you do that you'll be goin' close to the graves."

"I don't think you guys are qualified to tell us where we can and can't go, if that's what you're trying to do," the foreman said. "Besides, what are you doing putting graves out in the middle of nowhere for, anyway?"

"It isn't the middle of nowhere," Nestor said. "It's where our people used to live."

"I've worked on a few thousand miles of road over the years but I never thought I'd see the day when I'd hear anything like this. You guys come in here telling us about graves we've never heard of, and we've already got our preliminary approvals and permits stapled to the wall. There isn't one word about there being any graves out there. Forestry didn't say dick about any 'graves'."

"Forestry doesn't know about them," Nestor said. "Nobody lives in that area anymore. Nobody knows about them but us."

"You're trying to tell me that there's graves out there but nobody knows about them."

"We know about them," Allan said.

"You just finished saying that Forestry doesn't know about them," The Suit said. "It's their job to know about *everything* that's going on out there."

"They don't know about the graves," Nestor said.

The foreman smirked. "Do you guys expect us to believe this horseshit? Give me a break!"

"This is a little strange, to say the least," KhakiPants said. "How is it that you fellas know about these graves but Forestry doesn't?"

"It's our land. Not Forestry's," Allan said. He stormed out of the trailer and slammed the door behind him.

"What's up his ass?" the foreman said.

Leonard leaned toward him. "You are."

"Well, I can tell you this much. I don't know how he expects to get anything accomplished when he keeps taking off."

"It's Forestry's responsibility to know what's going on out in the bush," The Suit said. "That's the status on that."

The foreman opened the door. "I think this little get-together's over."

9

They sat around the fire in camp. "I wonder who that other guy was?" Nestor said. "The guy with the suit."

"Must be a bigshot from Timbco – the lumber company runnin' the show."

"What got into Allan? He's taken off twice now," Dayton said.

"He'll show up when he's ready," Nestor said.

"Do you think it would help if ya talked this over with the old boys? Maybe they'll have some suggestions."

"It's hard to say, but I can talk to them. I think it would be good if you'd come out to the lake sometime. The old fellas aren't comfortable around strangers but once they get to know you a bit they'll know who I'm talking about when I mention your name."

"Whaddya say, Dayton? Do ya mind if I use your truck?"

"Can't Nestor just tell them what's going on? I don't see why you have to be there."

"I'd like to get to know 'em, like Nestor was sayin', so they can put a face to a name when they're talkin'."

"Yeah, all right."

"I'll run out in a day or two," Leonard said.

"That would be good," Nestor said. "I have to send a package to Edmonton. The bus is going to be at the gas station pretty soon so I better get going." He jumped into his truck, turned it around and headed out to the highway.

Dayton went into the tent and returned with a can of fruit cocktail. "You don't really care about all that stuff, do you?"

"I do, as a matter o' fact. I grew up in an area where the native community wasn't shown much respect. I didn't think much of it when I was back home because I was a lot younger then and didn't recognize what was goin' on. Since I quit drinkin' I've been seein' things differently than I did before. Now it's easier for me to see where there are too many white footprints. This might be one of 'em."

"I'm surprised how friendly you're getting with those guys. Allan's sure weird, though."

"I think I know where he's comin' from — where ya don't want to talk to anybody or see anybody. I think he might have had a few challenges in the past. I can relate to that 'cuz I've been there."

"You're just wasting your time, as far as I'm concerned. We're supposed to be fishing."

"I want to go fishin' as bad as you do. How about we go back to the beaver dam tomorrow? We can head out first thing in the morning."

10

A tall stack of pancakes covered with tin foil sat in a plate near the coffee pot.

"Do ya want cackers?" Leonard said through the tent to Dayton.

"Do I want *what*?!"

"Cackers. Cackleberries. *Eggs*."

"Yeah, okay."

In half an hour they had eaten. Leftover pancakes were stuffed into an empty bread wrapper, thermoses were filled.

By midmorning Dayton had caught four brook trout, doubling Leonard's catch. Opening his thermos, Leonard poured strong black coffee into his cup and walked along the edge of the beaver pond, warding off mosquitoes with one hand, leveling his cup with the other. He stopped at the crest of a small knoll. Green marmalade of muskeg spread to the north and west. The hill was a wart on the horizon. Squinting, he focused on a man slopping knee deep through the muskeg toward the river.

Dayton had two fish cleaned by the time Leonard got back to the lean-to.

"You saw that guy, eh?" Dayton said. "I was watching him with your binoculars. He was packing a lot of gear."

"I can think o' better ways of spending my time than walkin' through that crap."

They had fried trout and cold pancakes for lunch. Dayton stretched out on thick sphagnum moss. "I'm going to take a nap. It's too hot to fish and the mosquitoes are driving me crazy."

"I'm gonna climb to the top o' the ridge. I might see a moose out there somewhere."

It was a short but steep climb. He followed a game trail, stopping several times to look and listen. He returned to camp several hours later. He tied a spinner onto his line and tightroped along a half-submerged log, casting the hook out into deep water. By early evening they had caught and released over thirty fish.

It had been a long time since he had enjoyed himself so much. He hunkered down at the lean-to and rolled a smoke. "I wonder where buddy there was headed," he said. "Sloggin' through the muskeg."

"He must be crazy. All he had to do was go around and he would of ended up here."

"He must be campin' out here somewhere. I imagine there must be a few people who come out now and then to do a little fishing or berry pickin'."

Dayton pulled off his boots and tossed them into the lean-to. "Maybe it's the guy that built the lean-to but he saw us here so he's going somewhere else. I don't know why anybody would leave their axe and shovel and all this other stuff out here, though. I'm surprised nobody's stolen it."

"I think it's got to do with the law o' the land. Anybody who comes here is welcome to use all this stuff as long as the firewood's replenished and the tools are put under the tarp when they leave."

"I came here to fish, not chop firewood all day."

Leonard lit the smoke. "Muskeg Marty must be dryin' off his boots by now."

"Who's Muskeg Marty?"

"The guy I was just talkin' about. The guy we saw in the muskeg. He'll likely be sittin' behind a fire right about now, maybe suckin' on a cool one, his boots danglin' from a couple o' pegs he's pounded into the ground. He'll be leanin' back thinking about what a great day he's had slogging through muskeg up to his knackers, wondering if it's all worth it and why he isn't down in Mexico someplace instead, drinkin' Tequila and lookin' at all the pretty senioritas. And all the while a grizzly with teeth the size o' pliers is lookin' him over from just around the corner, sizin' him up, thinkin' how tasty he'd be right about now, having marinated himself in warm beer."

"It sounds to me like *you're* marinated."

"When I was younger I could sit in the bar all night. I could drop a dozen beers faster than I could pay for 'em. And I'd get up at six in the morning and go to work rakin' asphalt all day. I was a tough bugger in those days. Can't do it anymore, though. Now I have to get up in the middle o' the night for a pee if I have a Coke watchin' Saturday night hockey."

11

Leonard parked the truck and crawled under it, oblivious to the rain-soaked grass he was lying in. "You're gonna need a good grease job pretty soon."

"How much is that going to cost?"

"A few bucks. I can do it right here. Won't take but an hour." Leonard crawled out from under the truck and brushed the mud off his jacket.

"You've been gone all day," Dayton said. "I thought you got stuck."

Leonard kicked a plastic pail toward the fire, turned it over and sat down. "It was an interesting visit. Nestor was right about the old fellas. They're pretty quiet. The one old boy kept grinnin' all the time and I don't think he understood a word I was sayin'. Nestor had to translate everything so I could get an idea of what they were talkin' about. They seem to be a couple o' decent old guys, anyway. The main thing they were concerned about was why we were interested in all o' this."

"You're the one that's interested, not me. I'm interested in getting some relaxation. So what's happening? Are you going to show them where the graves are?"

"The way Nestor explained it the old boys agreed to go to the roadcamp because they want to see where the road's plotted on their maps. It sounded good to me because Allan wants the roadboys to be aware o' the fact that if a couple of old men are concerned about where the road's gonna be goin' they'll realize how serious this is to 'em."

"It's not going to do any good, if you ask me. They probably don't even know how to read a map."

"If ya don't mind my usin' your truck I'll run up to let Slick and the roadboys know they can expect a visit from the old fellas in a day or two. I'll go to the lake afterwards and tell Nestor that a meeting has been set up and they should all plan on makin' a little road trip in a couple o' days."

Dayton dug into his sweatpants and pulled out a five dollar bill. "If you're going to be driving all over the country you may as well stop at the gas station and get me a bag of Potato Krisps."

12

A topographical map and several aerial photos covered the office table. Leonard placed his thumb on the map. "This whole area in here's muskeg. If a bulldozer gets stuck in there you might not get it back out."

"We've got equipment big enough to pull a house down," Slick said.

The Suit pointed to a large wall map. "At this point Forestry has only given us approval to go to the edge of the muskeg. There are some Special Areas farther back they won't let us into. We're going to have to take a look at the possibility of detouring south."

Allan and the old boys were standing in a corner. "As long as you stay away from the hill," Allan said. "It's sacred ground around the hill."

"*Now* what are you talking about?" the foreman snapped. "The other day you said that there were a couple of graves out there. Now you're trying to tell us that all around the hill is sacred ground. I think you're making this up as you go."

Nestor spoke. "The whole area is sacred ground. The centrepoint is the crest of the hill."

"I don't believe this," Slick said. "Is it marked? How is anybody supposed to know where it is?"

"If you have a pencil I can mark it in."

KhakiPants pulled a red pen out of his shirt pocket. Nestor circled the area around the hill.

The Suit stepped up. "Are you trying to tell me that somebody went out there and marked out what you're calling a boundary when about the only thing they owned was a bow and arrow?"

"When I saw that fancy suit o' yours I figured ya might be a reasonable man," Leonard said. "How about ya be reasonable enough to give us fifteen minutes outside?"

"I haven't got all day."

They were back in five minutes.

"The old fellas think it would be disrespectful to have heavy equipment go in and break the sanctity of the sacred ground. They would like to see the boundary re-established."

The Suit stepped toward him. "If you think we're going to spend money to survey a boundary we don't have any use for, you better think again."

"It's our land," Allan said.

"What the hell are you talking about – *your* land!" Slick snapped. "Can you see anywhere on the map where it shows that there's an Indian reserve?"

"It's Indian land." Allan paused. "It's s*acred* land."

"You're going to have to detour the muskeg," Leonard said. "You don't have to be a rocket scientist to figure that out."

The Suit pointed to the door. "You can all leave."

Nestor went out to his truck with the old boys. Leonard approached a few minutes later.

"Allan left again," Nestor said. "We were wondering if we should try to catch up with him."

"Let's park the trucks up the highway on the other side o' the hill. We can talk."

Nestor and the old boys climbed into Nestor's truck. Leonard followed them out to the highway and over the crest of the hill. They parked in the ditch. The old boys sat on the tailgate. Leonard and Nestor hunkered down in a poplar stand.

"What's on your mind, Leonard?"

"I've been givin' it a lot o' thought the past few days, and I think it might be best to show the roadboys where the graves actually are."

"I don't know how well that would go with the others. Kawatina means a lot to them. The old fellas grew up with it. They have family there."

"If we show the roadboys where the graves are they'll know we're not makin' any o' this up. They'll see with their own eyes that we're bein' up front with 'em."

"I'll talk to them. But I don't know what they'll say."

They walked back to the trucks and headed out.

13

Leonard looked into the sideview mirror of the truck. Pulling a towel from around his neck, he wiped the shaving cream off his face. "Shaving is a pain in the butt."

"Where's Allan these days?" Dayton said.

"Good question. I'm gettin' a little worried about him."

Nestor pushed a file into the blade of an axe. "Don't worry about Allan. He'll show up when he's ready."

"Did you get a chance to talk to the old fellas about showing the roadboys where the graves are?"

"We talked all night about it. They know this country well because they grew up in it. They've seen how things have changed over the years. They know from what they've seen that there isn't much we can do to keep anybody away from the graves unless we approach Forestry or Indian Affairs about it. But they don't want to do that. They agree with what Allan says – the fewer people who know about Kawatina, the better. They said that as much as they would like to see the location of the graves be kept secret it would be sensible to show the roadguys where the graves are, so we would have the assurance they won't be disturbed by any heavy equipment. But they made it clear they don't want Forestry involved."

"I don't imagine Allan's gonna be too thrilled about it."

"He won't be," Nestor said. "He doesn't think the oil companies should be allowed to come up here and tear everything to pieces when the only people who are going to benefit from it are the shareholders of the oil company. When they finish a job they pull out and leave, and the local residents are left with putting everything back in order. A lot of people, not just First Nations, feel the government hasn't regulated industry in the forested areas thoroughly enough. And when you see what's going on in the industry it's clear that big oil is essentially telling the government what it's going to do, and in the end the government okays it. Another thing I think is bothering Allan is that he feels you guys are getting involved in something you don't have any connection to."

"He's right," Dayton said. "We came up here to fish but we're spending a lot of time with this Indian stuff."

"I think there's more to it than calling it 'Indian stuff'," Leonard said. "To me it feels like we've made a discovery, like some kind of archeological find. I think we owe it to Allan, for one, and to the people who are resting there, to see they get the respect they deserve. I think we should do what we can to help out."

"What's in it for us?" Dayton said.

"I'll feel good knowing we helped out, somehow."

"I'm worried about how Allan is going to react if we tell the roadboys where the graves are," Nestor said.

"Maybe we should talk to 'em again. You can answer any questions they might have come up with."

"That probably wouldn't hurt. When would you want to go?"

"Whatever's good for you is good for me."

"I think we should wait a day or two. It looks like it's going to rain again. The road into the lake gets pretty greasy and I might not be able to get out in two wheel drive. Allan should be back soon. I'll talk to him about what we discussed and we'll come back here and let you know what we've decided. It would probably be a good idea to let the roadboys know we'll be back in a few days to talk to them." Nestor snapped up the tailgate. "I better get going." He pulled out of camp.

Dayton crouched at the fire as Nestor headed toward the highway. "I think you should forget it. This is way over your head."

"I've got Indian blood in me so I can understand how they feel about what's goin' on. Kawatina is a cemetery, when you get right down to it. I'd probably be a little upset if I saw a bulldozer rumbling through the cemetery in Kroywen. A place of rest is a place of rest. It doesn't matter where it is. Every race o' people has its own way of dealing with those who have passed on, but there should always be respect for the dead, no matter what colour their skin is or what part o' the world they live in."

14

The coffee pot rested against a rain-soaked log. Nestor, running toward the tent, stopped at Dayton's truck and jumped in. He honked the horn.

Leonard's head protruded from the tent. Nestor got out of the truck, slipped on wet grass and fell. Picking himself up, he scrambled to the tent. Leonard pulled him in and closed the flaps.

"Some storm, eh?"

"I haven't seen a storm like this in years." Nestor pulled a jackknife out of his jacket and scraped mud off his jeans.

"There was a bolt o' lightning last night must've been thirty feet from the tent." Leonard pulled on a raincoat and opened the tent flap. Wet wind whipped his whiskered face. "According to the weather forecast it's gonna be kind o' nasty all week. How did ya make out? Is Allan back?"

"Yes. But he's not happy. He doesn't like the idea of having to show anybody where the graves are. We talked for a long time. He reminded me of what happened several years ago when there was some oilfield activity on a reserve not far from here. The company doing the work didn't do a very good job of cleaning up before they left. In the spring, after the snow melted, there were oil cans and cardboard boxes and bits and pieces of garbage all over the place. A land man was sent out and the band was paid a few hundred dollars to cover the cost of the cleanup. Allan doesn't want to see something like that happen with Kawatina – the road guys assuring us they're going to do everything above board, to make it look good, but in the end not doing it. He said he doesn't want you to be involved when we talk to the roadguys. He wants to be sure they understand what's going on, but he doesn't think you're close enough to it." Nestor unscrewed the boots from his feet, pulled off his socks and wrung them out through the opened flap. "I walked in from the highway. Allan's back in the truck."

"We better go get him."

Nestor wrestled the socks back onto his feet and tied up his boots. They ran out to Dayton's truck. Pounding through deep water holes out to the highway, Leonard pulled up beside Nestor's truck. "We've got a pup tent in the back. What do you think of the idea of me and Dayton staying out at the lake for a couple o' days? This might be a good time for the whole works of us to get together and get to know each other a little better."

"I don't think the old boys are interested in having Dayton get involved in any of this. From what I hear, Allan's been telling them he doesn't trust Dayton. They don't have a problem with you because Allan told them they could trust you. But I think it would be better if we left Dayton out of this. Allan wasn't very anxious to come out today because he knew Dayton would be here. I had to talk him into it. But we can take Allan to the lake and I'll come back here with you."

"Sounds like a good idea. Get into your truck and I'll go back and tell Dayton I'm gonna follow you back to the lake."

Leonard returned to camp and honked the horn twice, waiting until Dayton had untied the tent flaps before scrambling in.

"Where's Nestor and Allan?"

"Back at their truck."

"I thought you said you were going to bring Allan back here."

"He isn't in a very good mood this morning. He's sleepin' in the truck. They're gonna go back to the lake but I don't know if they'll make it in two wheel drive. I told Nestor I'd follow 'em back in case they hit the ditch. Nestor's gonna come back with me and spend the night here."

"Why don't you go to the roadcamp now?"

"I think Nestor wants to get Allan back to camp first. Allan said before that he wanted to be with Nestor when he talked to the roadboys but I think he's changed his mind. We'll get him out to the lake and come back in my truck. Your truck. We'll talk to the roadboys later on."

15

Leonard crawled out of the tent. Nestor, sitting at a small morning fire, pulled at a thick woolen blanket draped over his shoulders.

"Mornin' Nestor. How are ya today?"

"I've got a bit of a chill this morning. This damp air seems to seep right into your bones."

"Get a little more coffee in ya. That'll help. I think our visit with the roadboys went pretty good, all things considered. KhakiPants sounded seriously interested in going out to see the graves."

"He must be under quite a bit of pressure from the Timbco people because there's only a mile and a half or so of road built. With all the rain we've been getting they've had more down days than production days. And now they have the muskeg to deal with."

"Sounds like Slick isn't comin'."

"The way they were talking he has some welding to do on one of the pieces of equipment and it has to be done right away." Nestor went to the back of the truck. "I've got something here for you." He handed Leonard a water bag. "Labrador tea. The old fella you call Grin made it for us for the trip. It'll give us some extra energy when we're walking. What about Dayton? Has he made up his mind yet whether or not he's coming?"

"He hasn't said anything, but I doubt it. He said KhakiPants dropped by yesterday when we were at the lake and asked him if he wouldn't mind running into Peace River to pick up a grader operator at the bus station. I think he likes that idea better than trudgin' through the bush all day."

"Is he working for the road crew now?"

"I'm not sure what's goin' on. The other day he mentioned he stopped in at the roadcamp to see if they had any lantern fuel they would sell him and they went to the kitchen for pie and coffee. KhakiPants told him he'd see about getting him one o' their old company trucks for a good price if he wouldn't mind doin' a little running around for 'em. That's probably what's happening now – the thought of getting a cheap company truck will get him kissing KhakiPants's ass. How's your truck runnin'?"

"It runs pretty good. But I wouldn't mind having a four by four." Nestor looked down the rain-drenched trail. "Seeing as how we aren't going to the graves until tomorrow and you're stuck with me for the day how about we clear out a few more willows from the trail?"

"I'll put the axe to work when it dries out a bit. There's no point in both of us gettin' wet when we don't have to. Besides, there's half a pot o' coffee left."

16

A drop of perspiration clung to KhakiPants's nose. "This would be a lot easier on horseback, wouldn't it? Whatever possessed you guys to come all the way back here?"

"Fish."

It had been tough hiking. The trails were wet and made walking difficult. They stopped once, for cold tea. Nestor had spoken only once all day. When they reached the gravesite area he turned and faced KhakiPants. 'This is Kawatina' was all he said.

They returned to camp as darkness fell. Dayton was sitting at a large fire. His hands, intertwined, rested on his bulbous stomach. "It's about time you got here."

Leonard leaned over a large pot in the fire. "That smells good."

"It's compliments of the road crew."

"It's a little something we thought we'd contribute," KhakiPants injected. "You fellas are roughing it out here and you're basically our neighbours so we thought it might be a nice change if you had a good, home-cooked meal. We've got one of the best camp cooks in the business."

"The foreman brought it out," Dayton said. "We had a good visit." He went to the truck and returned with an armload of folding chairs. "The foreman said there were a bunch of these taking up space in the storage trailer."

Leonard took the top chair and unfolded it, seating himself at the fire.

"How did my truck get here?" Nestor said.

"When I got back from the roadcamp this afternoon it was parked here."

"Allan must have dropped it off. He's likely camped somewhere nearby."

KhakiPants untied his laces and pulled wet boots from his feet. "I'm so hungry I could eat my boots!"

After everyone had finished eating, bowls and spoons were plopped into a bucketful of water. KhakiPants spoke up. "Is there anything else we can help you fellas out with?" He pulled a toothpick out of his shirt pocket and used it to clean a fingernail. "I think we've got a four burner propane stove in the equipment shed someplace. Why don't I bring it out some time?"

"We don't need it," Leonard said. "We've got enough firewood here to last 'til Christmas."

"It would be kind of nice to set up in the tent when it's raining, wouldn't it? You could make coffee and heat up something to eat without having to worry about trying to get a fire going."

"I think that's a good idea," Dayton said.

Nestor stood up. "I should be getting back."

"Do you have to go already?" KhakiPants said. "I thought we could talk a bit."

"I'll walk ya to your truck," Leonard said.

"I think we have something else that might interest you, Dayton," KhakiPants said, "but I can't say too much about it here. And we might have a little running around for you to do if you're interested."

Nestor's truck broke the silence. Leonard returned several minutes later.

"His truck *sounds* like an Indian truck, doesn't it?" KhakiPants said.

"He cracked the exhaust manifold last week."

"I wonder why the other native fella didn't stay here when he brought the truck out?"

Dayton waited for Leonard to answer.

"Allan's pretty quiet."

"I kind of picked up on that when you fellas were at the office." KhakiPants tightened his bootlaces. "I'm tired! I feel like I could sleep for a week. Anything we can help you out with, fellas, just let us know." He headed toward his truck.

"What about the stewpot?" Dayton said.

"Bring it to camp when you're done with it. There's no hurry." KhakiPants turned his truck around and drove out to the highway.

Dayton belched. "That was pretty thoughtful of them."

Leonard was urinating behind the woodpile. "Can't hear ya."

Dayton waited until he got back to the fire. "I think it was pretty thoughtful of those guys to bring all this stuff out."

"Yeah – they're a couple o' sweethearts."

"You were digging into the stewpot like the rest of us."

"I'll eat anything, as long as someone else cooks it."

"You don't want to give those guys a chance. I can't understand why you always have to be on their backs."

"I guess I don't play very well into their politics."

"What politics?"

"What's the fancy term they use for situations like this? *Quid pro quo?* Something like that. What it boils down to is that they scratch your back and you scratch theirs. That's the way it works. They're no dummies. Givin' us the stew and the chairs and the propane stove is all part o' doin' business. It's all part of getting their job done. I wouldn't particularly want to call 'em the greatest guys in the world just because they've given us a few goodies. It's all part o' doin' business."

"You're always looking for the negative side in everything."

"I beg to differ with ya, but in this case you're probably right. Most o' the thoughts I have o' those two are shrouded in a grey cloud. I'm gonna try walking the stiffness out o' my legs for an hour or so. I found a fox den near the highway the other day. I'm gonna poke around and maybe I'll see something." He went into the tent to get his flashlight. "Bye the bye," he said through the canvas, "that *was* good stew."

17

The sun hid behind the tops of the trees. A truck creaked along the trail into camp.

"Who would that be?" Dayton said.

"Must be Nestor. I told him I'd take a look at the U joint in his pickup."

A dirty white four by four stopped beside Dayton's truck. KhakiPants and the foreman climbed out. "Hello, hello," KhakiPants said. "We've got a little surprise package for you. There were four chickens left over from supper tonight and the cook thought maybe you fellas could take care of them."

"Sure. Would you like coffee?" Dayton said.

"Sounds real good." KhakiPants unfolded a metal chair and sat at the fire. Slick leaned on the truck. "It's too bad the native fellas are camped so far away. I'd like to talk to them. How far is their camp from here?"

"About an hour's drive," Dayton said. "But they're not very sociable."

"They haven't spent much time around white people. And they don't speak much English. That's all it is," Leonard said.

"Whaddya mean?" Slick said. "They speak perfectly good English!"

"The old boys don't speak English very often," Leonard said. "Nestor and Allan interpret everything for 'em."

"I don't care about the old guys," KhakiPants said. "I'd like to talk to the other two, though. The young fellas."

"Nestor said he might drop by sometime. I don't think he's comin' today, though. It's gettin' late."

"What do you fellas make of all that sacred ground stuff they're talking about? You don't believe it, do you? You'd think that if it really was sacred ground Forestry would know about it."

Leonard pulled out his tobacco. "A lot o' that kind o' stuff they keep to themselves. Aboriginals were in this country before it *was* a country, when they didn't have to be concerned about tellin' anybody much of anything. They don't talk about it 'cuz it's something that's private to 'em. The only reason we're involved in it now is because we discovered the graves by accident."

Slick fetched a chair, pulled it open and sat beside KhakiPants.

"Let's be realistic," KhakiPants said. "There aren't any graves out there. They want us to think those mounds are graves so we won't go near that area with our equipment. I think they like those big trees or something. Sometimes these natives get carried away with the 'traditional' stuff they always like to talk about because it sounds mystifying to a lot of people. They come up with stories about 'sacred ground' and 'spiritual' this and that when they're just looking for attention.

"There's a timber berth on the west side of the river that represents a lot of money and a lot of jobs. We're in a bit of a spot because we're limited to where we can put the road. There's a Critical Wildlife Area back there that no one's allowed into except on foot. On top of that we're going to have to detour the muskeg. We can follow some existing cutlines to the north but that will add more miles to the road, and the bean counters in Edmonton are always crying about extra costs. They're saying that if we use those existing cutlines we'll end up burning more fuel hauling the timber out. Burning more fuel means spending more money. According to scouting reports our surveyors have brought in the only way we're going to get to the other side of the muskeg is by detouring south, where the muskeg narrows. That could end up being near where their so-called graves are."

"They're real graves," Leonard said. "I dug up the headstones myself."

"Have you ever found an arrowhead? I found lots of them when I was a kid. You can go into most any museum in this part of the country and see hide scrapers and arrowheads and all sorts of old native artifacts. The stones you found are probably some rocks they used years ago for one of their cockamamie dances. We could probably go out there right now and find a dozen more of them if we dug around a bit."

It was obvious to Leonard that KhakiPants didn't show up with four freshly-roasted chickens out of the goodness of his heart. He was here on business. "How is it, then, that Nestor and Allan say they're graves if in fact they aren't?"

"Like I said, these people are always trying to impress us with their 'spiritual' mumbo jumbo. Nobody's going to try and tell me that just because you see a couple of humps in the ground you're looking at Indian graves."

"First Nations people were here long before the Vikings showed up. That's why they're referred to as First Nations. This is their land. Their nation. In days past, when they died they were taken care of by their families. Some of 'em were buried in the ground and some of them were placed in trees, but they were all put to rest respectfully, one way or another. Hundreds of thousands of First Nations people died in this country long before white men started showin' up. Long before there were shovels to dig graves or Christian crosses to mark 'em. For all we know there could be a hundred graves at the hill. But don't expect Nestor and Allan to tell you about 'em. This part of the country is full o' cutlines the oil companies carved through the bush when they were lookin' for oil. I'm havin' a little trouble understanding why you have to knock down so much good timber to build a road when you can use a lot of the cutlines that are already here."

"It doesn't matter what *you* think," Slick said. "You've got nothing to do with this operation."

"Well," KhakiPants said, "we've established that there aren't any graves out there. It's supposed to start raining again next week. We're meeting with the surveyors tonight to come up with a detour route around the muskeg. Timbco wants us to scout the area with a helicopter so we can plot on a map exactly where we're going to put it."

"I think I've heard enough," Leonard said. "Mind those little willow stumps on the trail when you leave. Ya might poke one through the sidewall of a tire."

Slick got into his truck and turned it around.

KhakiPants turned toward Dayton. "What are you doing tomorrow?"

"I've got a cramp in my leg that's been bothering me. I was thinking of going to town to get some salve or something for it."

"We have a First Aid room in one of the trailers. There's probably some kind of ointment in there that you can use. Now and then one of the equipment operators complains about a sore back so we need to have something on hand for stuff like that. Come by in the morning and we'll see what we can find for your leg. And we have a few other things we'd like to talk to you about." KhakiPants joined the foreman in the truck and they drove out of camp.

Dayton got the flashlight from the tent and walked down the trail a short distance.

"Leonard. Come here."

Leonard stuffed the tobacco pouch back into his shirt pocket and went over.

"There's a lot of sharp little stumps in here where you cut the willows off. I didn't realize it until you told them to be careful not to get one stuck in their tire. Is it like this all the way to the highway?"

"You tell me. You've been drivin' up and down here pretty well every day."

"I didn't know they could puncture a tire."

"It was my way of remindin' 'em to be careful about what they're doin', in an offhand kind o' manner."

Dayton headed for his truck. "I'm going to the gas station to put ten dollars worth of gas in, to make sure I have enough for tomorrow in case they want me to go somewhere."

"Ya better get movin'. Chap stays open late over the summer holidays but I think tonight's Bingo night, and Chap likes his Bingo."

Dayton pounded out of camp, oblivious to the willow spears he had been concerned about a few minutes earlier.

Leonard headed toward the fox den.

18

Dayton stopped the truck. "How long have you been cutting willows?"

"All day. I should have it cleared out in one more shift." Leonard bent a long willow over and swung at it with the axe. It snapped. "You and your buddies won't have to worry about scratching your trucks or puncturing tires." He climbed into the truck and they bounced back to camp.

"Where have ya been?" Leonard said, gathering kindling for the fire. "You left camp at six o'clock this morning."

"I woke up early and started thinking about what they said about wanting to talk to me. I couldn't get back to sleep so I went to Valleyview and had breakfast at the truck stop. After I ate I went to the roadcamp. They were talking about running an ad for some kind of engineer when I first got there. They were curious about what we were doing before we came up here. I told them I was the superintendent in a big condominium complex. They asked me if we were looking for work and I told them that it would depend on what the job was. There might be something for me in the Edmonton office later on, they said. The helicopter they were talking about showed up at noon, and after lunch we went out and did some scouting. They said that they're going to do everything in their power to get across the river as soon as they can because they've got some new state-of-the-art equipment they want to start testing."

"State-of-the-art equipment for what?"

"For knocking the timber down. It's new laser technology. I'm not supposed to say anything about it but I know you're not interested in any of this so I can tell you a bit about it. It's a truck or track-mounted doghouse that has a bunch of high-tech electronic equipment in it."

"Does it work?"

"They're working out the bugs now, but they said that the tests they've done with their research department have a lot of people interested."

"What's all the magic about?"

"It's fairly complicated. The operator sits in a doghouse, which is basically like the cab of a truck, and aims a narrow beam that's comprised of four individual beams at the trunk of the tree he wants to fall. He basically aims the beam at the trunk of the tree he wants to cut down and pulls the trigger of the beam gun. They showed me some samples of the logs they had cut with it. They want to have the ability to use it in any type of timber cover. They're talking about getting some big money partners involved. Later on they want to set up operations in South America. They asked me if I'd be interested in spending a year or two down there."

Leonard dug out his tobacco. "I can see where this thingamajig would eliminate the need for fallers. From what I can recall back east those guys can make a lot o' money in a day. I can appreciate their thinkin' in that if they can eliminate all these pricey fallers they'll show some bigger numbers in the profit column. But fallers are skilled craftsmen – they can drop a tree on target by makin' the right cuts. The doozlewhopper you're talkin' about doesn't know anything about lean, or wind, or whatever else you need to know to drop a tree accurately. What it looks like to me is you're gonna end up with a timber berth lookin' like a pile o' pickup sticks, with trees tangled every which way. They're gonna fall where the laws o' gravity and physics dictate where they're gonna fall."

Dayton had a sneer on his face. He defensively exuded a long, loud belch.

"I dunno how many branches there are on a tree but ya gotta think that on big fir there must be a hundred. So there are gonna be limbers with chainsaws crawling through all that crap on the ground, trying to trim 'em. I'm not a logger but I can see in my mind's eye a thousand trees lyin' all over the place and a bunch o' limbers doin' their best tryin' to figure out how to make their way through it all."

Dayton belched again.

"And you're gonna have to put up a steel spar in the middle of it all so you can drag the logs out. And you'll still need chokermen to snare the logs so they can be dragged down to the road for pilin'."

"This is new technology, Leonard. You don't come up with breakthrough technology overnight. It's people like you that are still back in the Middle Ages and aren't ready to try anything new."

Leonard went behind the woodpile to relieve himself. Returning to the fire he sat on thick, warm grass, spread his legs and looked into a quiet sky. "How much is this laser contraption worth, anyway?" *Contraption*. He liked that.

"They've put just under four million into it so far. The shareholders want to see timber come out of the bush, and the way to get the most timber out of the bush is to use state-of-the-art technology. That's the way Timbco looks at it. They've got some computer consultants coming up from the States to work in the Edmonton office to see if they can speed things up. They want to set up the equipment as soon as they get across the river so they can get everything fine-tuned."

"What if it doesn't work? What if they come up with a glitch they can't fix?"

Dayton went to the woodpile. He grabbed a piece of firewood, walked toward a big bam tree on the edge of the clearing and threw the firewood at a large black bird.

"That freakin' crow has been sitting in that dead tree since the day we got here."

"It's not a crow, it's a raven. I've been leaving scraps for it at the bottom of the tree."

"You were saying something about finding glitches in the laser logger. They'll get the bugs out. There's no doubt in my mind about that."

"Did you actually see 'em cuttin' a tree with it?"

"It's in Edmonton. That's where they're running the preliminary tests. There's going to be a shareholder demonstration when they get it finished. I put ten grand into shares. The way they were talking I stand to make close to a quarter of a million dollars when it's operational."

"Nothin' like a little inside information, eh?"

"Do you want in? I can get you set up."

"I'll pass. The way you're talkin' they want to get this thing set up in the timber berth as soon as they can."

"They're hoping that by the time the road crew gets to the river and they put a bridge in they'll have it working properly. They don't want to wait until the road is built all the way into the timber berth because they want to do their field tests with it as soon as they can. They said that Forestry wants to have a look at it. It sounds like they marked off an area west of the river where they can do the testing. I think you'd be a fool not to put some money into it. You've been getting screwed up with all this other crap. Between me and you, you're not very popular with the road guys. They're afraid that you might go to Indian Affairs or the Mounties and cause more delays. They're worried that they aren't going to get the road built in time because you're making a big deal out of the graves. They said that Timbco has been getting a lot of pressure from a few of the shareholders who have threatened to pull their money out if the road isn't finished by a specific date."

"I don't care what they do as long as they show proper respect for the sacred ground. What did the roadboys say about the graves?"

"Like they said before, what you guys are calling graves are just a couple of big trees that fell down years ago and got covered over with moss. We saw everything from the chopper. As far as they're concerned Kawatina doesn't exist and it never did."

"But you saw the graves yourself."

"No, I didn't."

"I marked 'em for ya with a plastic bag after we crossed the river when I went back to the gas station to look for the old boys."

"When you went ahead of me to mark the graves I didn't feel like walking around all day so I stayed at the river when you headed back to camp to get the truck. When they asked me if I had seen any graves I didn't lie to them. I told them I didn't see anything, and I didn't."

"KhakiPants saw them. I was there. We were standin' right beside 'em."

"As far as he's concerned they're just a couple of humps on the ground."

"And as far as *you're* concerned?"

"As far as I'm concerned if they don't think there are graves out there I'm not going to argue with them. I was with them all day. I think they want to hire me, and if I have a chance of getting on in the Edmonton office I'm going to agree with them. From what I could see from the chopper the road won't be anywhere near the graves, anyway."

"So you do admit there are graves over there."

"I could care less what's out there. All I know is that it sounds like they're going to offer me a job, and a job with a big company is a lot more important to me than a couple of Indian graves."

"It's none o' my business what ya do. As long as the roadboys aren't goin' near the graves they can think whatever they want to think. I told Nestor I'd help him sort some tamarack rails he's been gathering. He said he has quite a few of 'em he wants to take to Slave Lake. Any chance I can use the truck? I thought I might spend the night at their camp."

"When you have my truck all the time I can't do any running around for the roadcrew. If they're going to put me on full time I have to make sure I've got a vehicle or I'm going to be out of a job."

"One o' these days I'm gonna have to get on the bus and go down and get my truck so I won't have to be usin' yours all the time."

"That sounds like a good idea." Dayton dug the keys out of his pocket. "Maybe you should put some gas in it. I'm not sure how accurate the fuel gauge is."

Leonard drove to the gas station. Chap was whistling in a back room. Making his way around a stepladder, Leonard looked up at a brown patch staining the ceiling. He helped himself to coffee and sat in a plastic chair out on the veranda.

Chap joined him as he was rolling a smoke.

"It looks like we're in for the sunniest day of the summer, Leonard." Chap's face was red. Perspiration dotted his forehead. "What's up today? Headed to the lake to do a little fishing?"

"I'm goin' up to see the guys."

Chap sat on the wooden steps. The sun bounced off his shiny head. "According to what I hear it's supposed to be nice all week. I'll tell you, it sure makes a difference in sales when the sun's shining."

Leonard took a long drag and watched a butterfly flutter by. "I told Nestor I'd give him a hand with a load o' tamarack rails he wants to take to Slave Lake. It's gettin' to be a bit of a pain using Dayton's truck all the time. He's at the construction camp quite a bit and it sounds like they want him to run around pickin' up parts and whatnot. He's gettin' a little impatient with my always usin' his truck so I think I'm gonna go down and get mine in a few days." He finished off the smoke and got up to go inside. "Did I see a couple o' watermelons around here someplace?"

"They came in yesterday."

"I better get one."

"How's your tobacco?"

Leonard dug into his shirt pocket. "I better get one o' them, too."

"You don't have to pay me now. I'll start a tab for you."

Leonard scooped up a watermelon, turned to leave and walked into the ladder.

"One of these days I'm going to have to get up in the attic and see if I can plug that hole."

"Maybe you won't have to worry about it anymore. Maybe it's gonna stop rainin'." Leonard headed for the door.

It took over an hour to get to the lake. Nestor was pulling a long tamarack rail from a pile half the height of the tent when Leonard pulled up.

"That looks a lot like work. You must be planning on havin' quite a little get-together."

"I like to bring a load to Slave Lake every summer, and whoever needs them can help themselves."

"Are you the only one here?"

"The others went down to Whitecourt."

"Are ya pullin' out the good ones?"

"I ended up getting quite a few so I'm weeding out the worst ones."

They spent several hours examining the rails, keeping the best ones for the teepees, piling the rejects at the woodpile.

"I made some cold tea this morning," Nestor said. "I'll get it out of the water and we can take a break."

Nestor fetched the tea, grabbed two cups from the table on the way back and sat cross-legged beside Leonard. "Something tells me you didn't come here to sort tamarack rails all day."

"I told you I'd give you a hand. Are they gonna spend the night in Whitecourt? I can come back tomorrow."

"I wouldn't be surprised if they show up any minute. Allan's their chauffeur for the day."

"I can't help but think the old boys are concerned about the possibility of the road detouring through the sacred ground."

"They have their concerns because they know that if the road has to detour south it will go near the graves."

"Maybe what we need is more people like Allan – to keep 'em on their toes."

"I'd like to see more young native people show an interest in our culture. It's slipping away from us. Things have changed a lot since I was a kid. Young people nowadays are getting tied up with all the high-tech stuff. I guess the bottom line is that it's more fun to play video games than learn how to tan a deer hide."

"I know what you're sayin'. It seems like almost any kid nowadays can master the most complex computer games but they have no idea where the 'start' switch is on the lawn mower." Leonard tilted his head and stood up. "Sounds like a three hundred and sixty cubic inch Ford with a cracked manifold comin' our way."

Nestor looked in the direction of the road. "They're back."

Allan parked in front of the tent. Grin went directly to the fire. Old George, holding onto his baggy brown pants, hustled over to a plywood outhouse.

"How are ya today, Allan?" Leonard said.

"I've got a headache." He went to the tent.

"He's not used to being in vehicles," Nestor said.

"That cracked manifold might have somethin' to do with it. There's probably carbon monoxide leakin' into the cab."

Leonard handed Grin the willow handle cup he had been using.

Grin grinned. "*Eh* heh."

Leonard pulled the truck keys out of his pocket. "I better get out of here."

"You don't have to go. If you don't mind giving me a hand cutting up the culled rails for firewood we'll go out a little later and see if we can catch a walleye or two for dinner. You may as well spend the night here."

George returned from the outhouse, filled the washbasin and took off his shirt. A long, jagged scar stretched from his shoulder blade to his hip. After giving himself a sponge bath, he went into the tent and came out wearing a clean, identical flannel shirt.

By early evening half the discarded rails had been lopped into two foot lengths. Old George stacked them onto the existing woodpile. Grin lay on his cot, watching a long legged spider crawl back and forth across the roof of the tent. They sat around a large fire for several hours before calling it a night.

It was early when Leonard stuck his nose out of the sleeping bag. The sun hadn't yet climbed the trees. Pulling a tarpaulin off his sleeping bag, he rolled both up and tossed them into the back of the truck. A pine squirrel, annoyed at having been interrupted so early in the day, scolded him through the trees. He pulled a handful of birch bark out of the tinder box and began building a fire.

"How did you sleep last night?" Nestor asked.

"Mornin'. I had a good sleep."

They took their time cutting rails in a cool blue morning, stopping occasionally to chat. It was almost noon when a crew cab truck penetrated the far end of the clearing.

"Looks like Slick's truck."

The truck stopped behind Nestor's. Three men climbed out. Dayton led the way. KhakiPants and Slick followed. The Suit remained inside.

"Forestry was out to see us," Dayton said. "They told us they would look at the possibility of giving us the okay to cross the muskeg at the narrow point at the south end. When we were out in the chopper we looked the whole area over. As far as we're concerned, Kawatina doesn't exist."

KhakiPants approached Leonard. "Those weren't graves you showed me. They were overgrown logs. There aren't any graves out there and there never were."

Slick stepped toward Leonard. "You and your friends here have to be some of the most ignorant people I've ever seen. If you think for one minute that you're going to stop us, you better think again." He pointed at Grin. "*That* dozy old bugger doesn't know if it's day or night."

The tent flap opened. Allan stepped out and stood in front of Dayton.

"Kawatina doesn't exist," Dayton repeated.

Allan gobbed a mouthful of snuff onto Dayton's shirt. "You treat the bush like you own it. But you don't."

"Just a minute now," KhakiPants said. "We can't knock down any trees until we have the proper permits. Everything has to be above board before we can take the equipment out of the yard. It takes months, sometimes years, to get everything in order before we can start work on some projects. You better be careful about what you're saying until you know all the facts. I'm glad we took the time to come out here, so we can get a few things cleared up.

"The first thing you have to understand is that we're here to build a road. The weather hasn't been very cooperative, but we're doing everything in our power to get some work done. Another thing that's creating a challenge for us is the muskeg we're all well aware of. You fellas were right – I'll give you credit for that – it's too soft out there to put any heavy equipment into. We're going to have to detour the muskeg, and we have two choices, two routes we can take. We can go south, to the narrow end of the muskeg near what you fellas refer to as 'the ridge'. But if we cross there we could be encroaching on what you refer to as sacred ground.

"We're aware Forestry might place some special restrictions on the south route if they become aware those 'graves' of yours are out there. To our understanding they aren't aware of them at this point. And you don't *want* them to be aware of them. So as far as we're concerned, and as far as Forestry knows, there aren't any graves out there. We've had our surveyors look for an acceptable detour. And we're here to tell you that we've found a route that skirts the muskeg by following a series of existing cutlines to the north. It's going to be longer than we prefer but it's on high ground and we won't have to spend as much time clearing bush because we'll be using existing cutlines. So that's the plan. That's what we're going to do. We have to be going now. We have things to do in Peace River."

The roadboys climbed into their truck, drove to the far edge of the clearing and out of sight.

19

Dayton poked his head out of the sleeping bag. "Leonard. Are you awake?"

"In a manner o' speakin'. I didn't get much sleep last night."

"The wind just about drove me crazy. I thought it was going to blow the tent over."

Leonard sat up in his sleeping bag. "I told Nestor I'd help him haul tamarack rails to Slave Lake one o' these days. I hope he doesn't want to do it today. I'm gonna have to go down and get my truck pretty soon so I don't have to be borrowin' yours all the time."

"That's a good idea. You're not covered on my insurance. They want me to pick up a portable power plant in Whitecourt pretty soon. They were wondering if you'd come with me to give me a hand. They said they'd pay you a hundred bucks."

"When's this supposed to happen?"

"They didn't know for sure. All they said was that they want to get a night shift going and they need the power plant so they can set up lights. So can you give me a hand? Like I said, there's a hundred bucks in it for you."

"How come there has to be two of us? I would have thought they'd use some kind of crane for the heavy stuff."

"They said they want two people to be there to make sure it gets loaded properly. If they want me to go down today are you going to be ready to go?"

"I don't see why not. Do you have any idea when the bus heads south out o' Whitecourt?"

"I have no idea. I'll tell them that we can be ready to go today." Dayton crawled out of his sleeping bag, got into his truck and headed for the road camp.

Leonard was into his third cup of coffee when he returned. He went directly into the tent and emerged wearing clean clothes.

"What's happenin'?"

"I'm going to Peace River to pick up one of the engineers. He was supposed to rent a car and drive to camp but they got some paperwork mixed up and there wasn't a car available for him at the airport."

"You didn't impress me yesterday when you showed up at the lake and started spouting off."

"I was trying to explain that whatever you have to say about the graves doesn't mean a thing to me or the road crew. Sometimes you have to come out and say certain things point blank. You get along pretty good with those guys but I've had my share of trouble trying to communicate with them."

"You've never really *tried* communicatin' with 'em. All I've ever heard ya do is bitch about the graves. I wouldn't call that communicatin'."

"The foreman told me that they have something they want to talk to you about. He wants you to go to the roadcamp as soon as you can. I can drop you off if you want."

"I'm ready when you are."

Leonard jumped out at the roadcamp. The office door was open. The Suit and Slick were sitting at the table. KhakiPants was standing at the window. He turned, facing Leonard.

"Good morning. We've been pretty busy lately trying to figure out a few things. We've come up with something we think you'll be interested in. We're under a lot of pressure to get the road finished. I'm sure you can understand that. I told the office that our best bet would be to use as many existing cutlines as we can, so we can keep costs down and stay on dry ground. Some hotshot down there thinks it's going to cost too much in the long run if we do it that way. There's about a mile of oil lease road we'd have to use." He pointed it out on the map. "That part's okay because it's that much less road we'd have to build. But we'd have to pay the oil company a user fee every time our trucks were on the road, and it would end up costing too much by the time the timber berth's logged out. The only choice we have is to cut our own road through the bush."

"You made it clear yesterday you were going to use existing cutlines. Instead o' knockin' down more trees. So what you told us was bullshit." Leonard leaned on the table and spoke directly into The Suit's face. "I'm about three eighths of an inch away from goin' to Forestry and tellin' 'em what's goin' on. There's been nothin' but bullshit comin' from you guys since day one. Dayton told me you had something important you wanted to talk to me about. But this is just more bullshit."

"We had a meeting last night," KhakiPants said. "We came to the conclusion that we're going to have to detour along the edge of the muskeg to the south end, where it narrows down, and cross it at that point. The people who you say are buried there will be moved so we can take out the fill we need to get across the narrow stretch of muskeg."

The Suit spoke. "We've had two concrete pods manufactured to put the bodies in."

"What are you talkin' about – *pods*?"

"They're airtight cement containers," The Suit said. "We'll dig up the bodies and put them in the pods so we can get them out of our way."

"Nestor and Allan are the ones you should be talkin' to. Not me."

"We've had a little trouble talking to the native fellas," KhakiPants said. "The younger fella seems to have a bit of a chip on his shoulder."

"If they were here now they'd tell ya to shove your friggin' pods where the sun doesn't shine. You know it and I know it. How do ya think you're gonna pull off this pod scenario without them knowin' about it? They'll be camped at the gravesite as soon as I tell 'em what's goin' on."

"We were hoping we could get you to help us out a little," KhakiPants smiled. "I told Dayton to look at a couple of good used trucks we have in storage in Peace River. We thought you might be interested in one of the better ones, if you'd be willing to help us out with this."

"I already have a truck. I'm goin' down to get it any day now."

"We're behind schedule," KhakiPants said. "We have to take advantage of every good day we get. We're going to be activating a night shift to get production up. Once we get through the muskeg we're going to have a portable bridge put across the river so we can angle the road north, into the timber berth. But we'll need good clay fill to get across that stretch of muskeg before we can put the bridge in. We'll get the Cats to go back and refill the borrow pit once the bridge is put in. Then we can move the bodies back to where they were before."

"If you dig a borrow pit you'll be usin' the clay from the pit. That's why it's called a borrow pit. And if ya move the bodies back to the original gravesites they'll be out in the open 'cuz you'll have cleared the bush away to dig the pit. It's just more bullshit."

"This is how it's going to go," Slick said. "We'll stay away from your burial area until we need fill to get across the muskeg. Then we're going to dig a borrow pit. I'm going to get the bulldozers to clear the whole area off. By the end of the day you won't be able to find a pinecone, let alone a grave. We'll get that area cleared off so smooth you can play pool on it. And if anybody asks us about seeing any graves we'll tell them that we don't know what they're talking about."

"Got a question for ya, Slick. How long do you think it would take you to get out to the graves and get everything shaved off, like you were just sayin'? If you jump on a Cat and head for the graves right now, how long do you think it would take? And if I phone Forestry and tell 'em there might be a little problem with the new loggin' road that's bein' built, who do you think would get to the gravesite first? You on your Cat, or me and the ranger in his truck?"

"If you think for a minute that we're going to kiss the ass of every fuckin' Indian that comes along, you better think again."

"As far as I'm concerned, you can kiss mine."

The Suit stood up. "It's time for you to leave."

Leonard left the door open behind him and walked back to camp.

It was early evening when Dayton returned. A large fire was burning. Leonard was sitting on the plastic pail, smoking a cigarette.

Dayton unfolded a steel chair and sat across from him. "What's the huge fire for?"

"The women."

"Is somebody here?"

"For the women out at the hill."

"Whatever." Dayton rummaged through a plastic bag and dug out a bag of potato chips.

"Did they say anything to you about cement pods when you saw 'em this morning?"

"I have no idea what you're talking about."

"The way they were talkin' they're going to detour south along the edge o' the muskeg and cross it at the narrow point near the south end. But first they're gonna dig up the bodies and put 'em in some kind of cement containers so they can dig a borrow pit to get the clay they'll need to get across the muskeg."

"Sounds like a good idea to me."

"What's up with the power plant they were tellin' you about?"

"It's supposed to be in Whitecourt in two or three days. They said they'll let me know when they want us to go down."

"Seein' as how there's no immediate panic I'm gonna go out to the beaver pond in the morning."

"I'm going to relax. I want to make sure I'm in shape in case they need me at the roadcamp."

"Nestor was here for an hour or so earlier on. He said he might come around again tomorrow. If he shows up, tell him I'm only gonna be at the beaver dam for a few hours." Leonard dug a ten dollar bill out of his jeans. "Next time you're in town, pick me up an inner tube if ya can. A bicycle inner tube."

"What are you going to do with a bicycle inner tube?"

"I've got a little project I've been thinkin' about."

20

"Here, Nestor. Have another one."

"I've had four pieces already. That's a lot of fish for a skinny guy."

Leonard scooped up the remainder of the trout from the frying pan. "When the roadboys came out to the lake they told us they were gonna use existing cutlines to detour north around the muskeg. But it was all bullshit. When I was at the beaver pond I ended up doin' quite a bit o' walking. I found survey markers all over the place. It turns out they're going to cross the muskeg at the south end, where it narrows down. The speech Khakipants gave us was a pile o' crap. The reason he went to the gravesite with us was so he could see exactly where the graves were. So they would have a better idea of what they were going to be headed into. I was at the roadcamp yesterday morning. They said they were going to dig up the graves and put the bodies in some kind of protective cement pods so they can relocate them while they dig a borrow pit to get the clay they need to fill in the narrow stretch of muskeg."

"I don't like that idea, Leonard. A lot of the Kawatina graves were here before the treaties were signed. It isn't right that they can come in and dig them up." Nestor paused in thought. "They told us they were going to do everything in their power to respect the gravesite. And the pods you just mentioned – I've never heard of anything like that before."

"I thought I'd better let you know what's happening. I think we should have a chat with our greasy-haired friend."

They climbed into Nestor's truck and headed for the roadcamp.

The foreman's truck was parked in front of the office. Leonard rapped on the door twice and they walked in. Slick, doing paperwork at the table, didn't look up. "I heard you coming," he said. "I'm busy."

Leonard sat across from him and clasped his hands together.

"Like I said. I'm busy."

"We can wait." Leonard started rolling a cigarette.

"There's no smoking in here."

Leonard pulled his chair in front of the open door and lit the smoke. Several minutes passed. Slick put his papers into the filing cabinet, brushed past Leonard, got into his truck and drove a hundred yards to the kitchen trailer.

Leonard and Nestor followed him. He was sitting at a table with the cook.

"You guys don't work here. Take a hike."

"There's something we want to talk to you about."

"I don't have time."

"We can wait."

"If you're looking for the Super, he's in Peace River."

"We're lookin' for you."

"When I finish up what has to be done around here I'll go to your little campsite. But don't hold your breath because I'm not in hurry."

Leonard scooped a loaf of bread from a tray beside the steps on the way out and stuffed it under his shirt. They went back to camp.

Slick pulled in half an hour later. "What's the big deal about wanting to talk to me?"

"I was out at the ridge yesterday. It looks like there's some kind o' survey markers out there."

"We already told you that if we go the south route we'll have to dig up some clay to fill in that narrow section of muskeg. We also told you that we'll move your so-called graves so we can dig a borrow pit to get the clay. If you think we're going to worry about a couple of bullshit Indian graves, you better think again. And I wouldn't think about talking to Forestry about it. They probably give as much of a shit about your graves as we do."

"The Forestry folks do other things besides watch trees all day. I'm aware of the fact they didn't spend a lot of time in school learning how to protect Indian graves, but it would be wrong to suggest they don't care about 'em. I'm sure they'd be concerned about the fate of a native gravesite if they knew there was gonna be some heavy equipment nearby."

Slick got into his truck and left.

21

"Heads up!"

Chap slid a bowl of ice cream down the counter. Opening a box of doughnuts, he put two on a paper plate.

"I knew I came to the right place when I came here," Leonard said. He jammed a doughnut into his mouth. Crumbs clung to his whiskers.

"What brought you fellas all the way up to this particular neck of the woods?" Chap said.

"I was laid off and I've always wanted to see this area so I thought it would be a good place to spend a little time fishing."

"What kind of work were you doing?"

"I was workin' in a garage. I'm a mechanic. The owner's rebuilding the shop so he shut everything down until sometime in the new year."

"If you're a mechanic you shouldn't have any trouble finding work."

"I've never had much trouble findin' work. But it's nice to get away from the fumes for a while. And I haven't been camping in years."

"What about your friend? What does he do?"

"He's a partner in a condominium complex," Leonard lied. "I guess his doctor told him to take some time off before he ended up havin' a heart attack. We got to talking and decided to come up here."

Chap went to the window. "How's the truck running?"

"It runs pretty good, considering Dayton doesn't do much maintenance on it, but I'm gonna go down and get mine in a day or two. Dayton's been runnin' around for the roadcrew, pickin' up parts and whatnot. He bought one o' their used trucks. He's drivin' it now. There's no insurance on this one anymore so he's gonna leave it parked in camp for the time being. I snuck it out so I could come here."

Leonard dug a five dollar bill out of his jeans and put it on the counter. "Do ya get the newspaper every day?"

"It comes on the bus every morning."

"Could you order a copy for me?"

"For tomorrow, you mean?"

"For every day."

***** ***** *****

It was dark when Dayton pulled into camp. He opened a can of pop and sat at the fire. "They want us to go to Whitecourt and load up the power plant in the morning."

"Good enough. I'll catch the bus there and go down and get my truck. The clutch is startin' to slip a bit so I might have to put a new pressure plate in it before I come back, but it'll only take a day to do that."

"There's a garage in Valleyview that the road crew uses now and then. If you told them it was one of the company trucks they'd probably give you some kind of deal."

"I'm not interested in any deals if it's with those yoyos. My money's as good as theirs. How would it be if I use your truck to run out to the lake? I wanna let the guys know I'm going to be gone for a few days in case there's something they'd like me to pick up when I'm in town."

Dayton pulled the keys out of his jacket pocket. "They've got their own trucks. They can go to town just as easily as you can."

"Their trucks are only two wheel drive. With all the rain we've been getting they've had to stay in camp most o' the time."

"They should get a four wheel drive then."

"You should sell 'em yours."

22

Leonard sat behind a dreary fire. Rainwater dripped from the trees.

Dayton pulled into camp, grabbed a grocery bag from the seat of the truck and joined him.

Leonard pulled a long drag from his cigarette. "They did quite a job out there."

"Out where?"

"Haven't ya been hangin' out with your roadbuildin' buddies the last couple o' days? You haven't been around here."

"I phoned them from Whitecourt after you left on the bus and they wanted me to pick up some paperwork in Edmonton. They said that I might as well spend a couple of days in the city to take a little break. I just got back from bringing them the paperwork. They said they were busy so I didn't have a chance to talk to them about anything."

"They dug the borrow pit when we were gone."

"Where did they put it?"

"At the gravesite. Like they said they were gonna do. They must have taken three acres o' trees out. It's flat enough in there to go bowling. I had to get the clutch in my truck fixed on the way up. I thought I could make it up here and do it myself in camp but it started slippin' so bad I could smell it. I took it into a garage on the highway. When I got back here you weren't around so I figured it wouldn't hurt to check things out at the river. It was raining by the time I got to the gravesite so I huddled under a tree along the edge o' the clearing they had carved out. I glanced back into the bush – and there was a finger pointin' at me. A human hand was danglin' from the branches of a tree.

"They dug up the graves as if they were cleanin' off a garbage pit. It was a hell of a mess. They pushed the bodies into a corner of the clearing and covered 'em with brush. There were more bones out there than you'll find in a twenty dollar chicken dinner. All they did was cover 'em up. Like a wild animal would do. I went back to the lean-to at the beaver pond and got the axe and bow saw so I could hack into the brush pile deep enough to find the main parts o' the bodies. When they were buried they were wrapped up in moose hide but most o' the bones had fallen out except the bigger ones. I had quite a time getting everybody stuck back together again."

"What do you mean, getting everybody stuck back together again?"

"The hip bone's connected to the leg bone and the leg bone's connected to the next one. I was slidin' around in gumbo all day. By the time I finished it was startin' to get dark but I managed to get 'em both put back together again. I've got them in a safe spot now, so they should be restin' a lot easier." He went to the woodpile and pulled a large coffee can out from under a log. He tossed it to Dayton. "Open it. Take a look."

Dayton pulled the plastic lid off the can. "What the hell is that?! And what are you doing with it?"

"It's Watina. Watina's hand. She was in one of the graves. She and her mother were both buried there, side-by-side. I thought maybe you'd like to get acquainted."

"What are you going to do with it? If Forestry finds out you've got it they might shut the road crew down."

"You wouldn't want that, would you? If the road crew gets shut down you might be out o' luck with the job you're gettin' all puffed up about."

"If they want to give me a job in their Edmonton office I'm sure as hell not going to turn it down for the sake of a couple of old Indian graves that have been out there rotting away. You're getting carried away with this and it doesn't have anything to do with you."

"They went into a place they had no business goin' into, and they know it sure as hell. The only reason you're goin' along with it is because you have the opportunity of gettin' in on some big bucks."

"I didn't come up here to get involved in any Indian grave bullshit. What I'm doing now is I'm getting my priorities established. If I end up in the engineering department with this outfit, that'll suit me just fine."

"I thought you had to have an engineerin' degree to be an engineer."

"They told me we can probably work something out."

"This is gonna blow Allan's mind. I gotta go."

"Where?"

"To the lake.   They have to know what happened."

23

Nestor and Allan were sitting at their fire. Old George was splitting firewood. Nestor got up when Leonard pulled into camp.

"Hello there. I see you got your truck."

"Yup."

Nestor opened the flap of a small wooden box and pulled out a coffee cup. He filled it and handed it to Leonard. "It looks like it's stopped raining for a while. You probably want to get out and do some fishing."

"I'll get out one o' these days. How's the truck runnin'?"

"I ordered an exhaust manifold from the auto wreckers. It's supposed to be in next week."

Leonard slurped at strong coffee. "I have bad news. They went to the river. With their equipment. They dug a borrow pit at the gravesite. They cleared the trees away with Cats and dug up the graves and ploughed out a borrow pit when Dayton and I were gone. We went to Whitecourt because the roadboys said they needed us to load up some kind o' power plant. But it never showed up. I got on the bus so I could go home and get my truck. It took longer to get back than I thought it would 'cuz I had to get a little work done on it. When I got back yesterday I could see that Dayton hadn't been in camp for a while, so I hiked over to the river. The only thing that's at the gravesite now is a big hole in the ground."

Old George said something in Cree.

"It's best you go now."

24

A pile of shavings sat at Allan's feet. He leaned against a boulder.

It would be different now. Another piece of perfect forest would be destroyed. The giant trees to the west and north would come down. Trucks would haul logs to the highway and beyond. They would be cut into planks at a new sawmill. City slickers would come out on the new road. To drink beer and get back to nature.

Pulling a wetstone out of his pocket he pushed a thin knife blade into it. He felt comfortable with its simplicity. But life wasn't simple. Things had changed. People had changed. They had allowed themselves to be drawn into something they had little control over.

Technology was in command. Everyone had a computer. With access to the worldwide web. They could email each other. They could be cool with the technology at their fingertips. It was the new way, Nestor had said. Technology was the new way.

The reports said technology would make life easier. But it didn't. It made it more complicated. Individuals forfeited their identities in order to be part of it. It sculpted their personalities and weakened their individualism. The people who ran things made it too easy for them to trade off their individuality for it. Technology controlled them.

Back in the day, white men arrived with their rifles and steel traps. They traded them for Indian furs. The native people came to rely on the white mens' technology. That was how it worked. That was how it was set up. They had the native people sign treaties they didn't understand. Then they took their land. They talked about how they would be more comfortable. They talked about how they would be independent.

They talked about a lot of things.

But that's *all* it was.

Talk.

25

Leonard yanked open the office door. KhakiPants and Slick were at the table.

"You said you were gonna put the bodies in those pods."

"What we do is our business and what you do is your business," Slick said. "This isn't any of yours."

"There was a time, as brief as it was, when I thought you were on the level when you said you were going to give Kawatina the respect it deserves. You told me you were going to put the bodies in those pod contraptions you were talking about. You dug up the graves, sure as hell, and I'd like to know where the pods are."

"That's our business."

"We're hoping to get Dayton fixed up with a job in our engineering department once we get this project finished," KhakiPants said. "I'm sure we could find you something, too. The pay's pretty good, I might add."

"I'll go to the soup line before I'll work for the likes o' you guys."

Leonard scrambled out of the office and got into his truck. Heavy, thick cloud had darkened the day. Light rain bounced off the hood as he drove to the gas station.

He parked beside the shop and walked over to the main building. "Anybody home?" He went to the back door and opened it.

"I'll be with you in a minute," Chap said. Sheets of wet wind blasted around him. He finished refilling a propane bottle.

Leonard went back inside, sat at the counter, rolled a cigarette and stuffed it behind his ear.

Chap fetched two doughnuts and coffee. Leonard took a doughnut off a paper plate and shoved half of it into his mouth. They sat with the blurry sound of rain around them and the splinking of water dripping from the ceiling into an empty ice cream pail beside them.

"Are you a licensed mechanic?" Chap said.

"I've got my interprovincial ticket."

"Did you say before that you might be looking for work?"

"I dunno. What's up?"

"I had a pretty good mechanic in the shop but he had to get half his stomach removed so he's pretty well finished as far as doing any heavy lifting goes. I've had a lot of people ask if I was going to get the garage going again. It's easier for them to come here than go to town. If you're interested maybe we can work something out."

"I just stopped in to pick up some tobacco. There's some bullshit happening out there and I want to get hold o' Dayton right away. We can talk about the job when I have a little more time."

The rain had stopped when Leonard pulled into camp. Nestor's truck was parked in the trees. Dayton was sitting under a tree, eating a hot dog.

"Nestor and Allan were here."

"I see that."

"They looked pissed off. Nestor said they're going to stay at Allan's lean-to tonight and come back in the morning."

"When I told 'em about the borrow pit they kicked me out o' camp." Leonard pulled the cigarette out from behind his ear, lit it and took a long drag. "They're not gonna be happy with what they see out there."

Nestor and Allan returned to camp the following afternoon. Allan went directly to the truck and pulled a snuff can off the dashboard.

"They laid some logs down to form two Xs near the borrow pit," Nestor said. "That must be where they put the bodies."

"I saw that, but no, it isn't. That's where they want us to think they put 'em."

"If they aren't there, where would they be?"

"I reburied 'em. I wanted to tell you that when I went out to see you. They had 'em covered over in a pile o' brush in a corner of the clearing. I dug 'em out and reburied 'em back in the bush."

"They told you they were going to rebury them in those pods," Nestor said.

"They had the pods built as an insurance measure, the way I've got it figured. That way they could go out there and dig the borrow pit and have their butts covered if Forestry found out they had dug up native graves. But they weren't even buried. They were shoved into a corner of the clearing and covered with brush. I scratched around in the pouring rain for the longest time before I found out that was where they'd put 'em. I think they were planning on settin' the brush pile on fire so everything would get burned up. But I didn't want to give 'em a chance to do that."

"*We* should have buried them."

"After I reburied 'em I dragged all the branches and whatnot that I'd cut from the brushpile out into the bush so it wouldn't look like anybody had been messin' around in there. It looks about the same now as when I found it."

Allan said something to Nestor in Cree.

"We'd like you to show us where you buried them," Nestor said.

"Of course."

Allan stood up.

"Now?"

Allan started walking.

When they reached the spur road leading into the borrow pit Leonard took the lead. He stopped at the edge of a poplar thicket.

"This is where I buried 'em. But they've been dug up."

Scuffling came from the bush behind them. Grin emerged.

"We should have brought some food," Leonard said. "For Grin."

"He's been camped out," Nestor said. "I've seen him go for days without eating."

"I'm gonna leave you guys be. I'm goin' back to camp."

26

A large teardrop of water clung to the ceiling and splinked into the ice cream pail.

"I'll crawl up into the attic and see about fixin' that hole."

"We patched up the roof before dad died. There's probably a pail of roofing tar out back in the house. If it's still there it won't take long to find it."

Splink

They went to the back door. A small grey bungalow sat in the corner of a neglected yard.

"That's a nice lookin' little house."

"It's the house I grew up in. I'm getting it torn down so we can put a modular home back here. I'm getting a little too old to be driving back and forth every day. I'll take a look in the cellar. We'll have to hurry because the gas truck's going to be here any minute."

The little house smelled of dust and old linoleum. Two open-jawed mousetraps sat beside the porch door.

"When are ya gonna tear it down?"

"In a month or so."

"It looks like a pretty solid house."

"It's probably one of the sturdiest houses around. Dad had fir planks hauled down from a mill his brother worked at. Go ahead and check it out if you like, but watch yourself going up the stairs – there's not much headroom."

"I can do that later. I'll go back and watch for the gas truck."

Dayton was sitting at the counter. "Good afternoon."

splink

"Good afternoon." Leonard got a coffee cup from below the counter, filled it for Dayton and refilled his own.

"It looks like I'm going to be moving. When I stopped in at the roadcamp there was a note taped to the office door. It said to meet them at the truck stop in Valleyview at noon. They took me out to a trailer court. They've got a trailer set up for me. *splink* They thought it would be more comfortable for me to live there than in the tent. The phone's already hooked up and they're going to pick up a TV in a couple of days."

"When are ya movin' in?"

"They still have to get the power and everything hooked up. In a few days, maybe."

"Chap offered me a job mechanicing."

"Are you going to take it?"

"It'll only take a few days to go down and get my tools rounded up, so I'm givin' it some serious thought. I told Nestor I'd put a manifold in his truck. Chap said he'd lend me whatever tools I need."

"Why don't you forget about those guys? That's all you've been doing is hanging around with them, helping them with everything."

"There's no point in 'em takin' the truck to a garage and spendin' all that money when I can get the parts and do it for 'em myself."

"For nothing."

"I don't need any money. Not from them."

"But the next thing you know the mechanic job will be taken by someone else."

"It won't take long to put the manifold in." Leonard held out his hand and intercepted a falling water drop. "I'm gonna crawl up on the roof and see if I can fix that leak."

"There you go again. That isn't your job. You don't even work here yet." Dayton went to the door. "I'll see you back at camp."

Chap came from the back, carrying a large pail. "I found it under a pile of shingles. I don't know if it's any good now, though. It's probably dried out." He tugged at the lid and pulled it open.

"It looks a little crusty. *splink* I've got a propane torch in the back o' the truck. We'll put some heat on it. I'll get up on the roof and you can stand on a chair and bang on the ceiling where it's leakin'."

"Before we get started, there's something I want to talk to you about. I overheard a bit about what you fellas were talking about. Your partner's moving to town, is he?"

"He's movin' into a trailer, by the sound o' things."

"I don't have a problem with you moving into the house if you're going to take the job. The power's disconnected and you'll have to use the shower in the shop, but once you sweep it up a bit I think it should be fine. Mind you, *splink* I'm going to be tearing it down, but you're welcome to use it 'til then." He went to the back room and returned with a few sheets of paper. "A little paperwork for you if you're going to take the job. All I need is the basic stuff – your social insurance number, place of birth, etcetera."

"How are ya gonna tear the house down?"

"A friend of mine has a breaking Cat. They use them for knocking down bush when they're breaking land. It's a bulldozer with a protective steel cage welded onto it to protect the operator. He's got a gravel truck and a loader and says he can have the house torn down and hauled away over a weekend."

"Seems like kind of a waste, tearin' down a perfectly good house."

"It's over sixty years old. I told my wife I'd build a new one years ago. She isn't too fond of mice, and we had a real run of them a while back. We had a mild winter and in the spring there were mice everywhere. We were looking at some modular homes at a show in Grande Prairie last spring. *splink* The wife likes the idea of a modular home because with this outfit you can change the floor plans and they'll build to your specifications and spot it for you. I'm glad we're going that route because I haven't swung a hammer in years. But yeah, the house out back is a great little house."

"Would you be interested in sellin' it?"

"I don't know that anybody would be interested in buying an old house that's been vacant for years."

"I'm kind o' thinkin' out loud here but if you could get it pried off the foundation you could set it up someplace else."

"I don't have the time, and once I get the shop going again I'll be too busy with other things. But like I said, you're welcome to live in it if you take the job. I've got all kinds of cleaners and disinfectants here. It wouldn't take much more than a day or two to get it cleaned up."

"I have a couple of other commitments that'll take a few days to clear up, but I'll give it some serious thought. I'll get the propane torch out o' the truck. We'll see if we can get that sealant softened up a bit. It shouldn't take much more 'n an hour to get the hole plugged."

Splink

27

"Hand me that crescent wrench, wouldja?"

"Where is it?"

"I'll get it." Leonard crawled out from under the truck. "It'll be nice when I get my tools up here. Ya can't do much with a crescent wrench."

Dayton threw a pop can toward the bam tree. "I wish that crow or raven or whatever it is would get lost. One of these days it's going to crap in the frying pan."

"I've been throwin' scraps under the tree to try and tame it a little."

"What are you going to do with that coffee can? Every time I take a leak I think about that hand. I don't know why you even brought it back here in the first place. Did you say Nestor was coming today?"

"He should be here any time. He's bringin' some tools from the shop so I can get his exhaust manifold fixed."

"Have you decided whether or not you're going to take the mechanicing job?"

"I don't think I'll have a problem workin' there atall. Chap said I can stay in the little house he has out back. He's gonna tear it down and put up a new one. I'm going to check it out and see how hard it'll be to get it off the foundation. I might even buy it."

"You always have to be doing something. We're supposed to be on a holiday."

"I spent a lot o' years wastin' my time and I've got a lot o' catchin' up to do."

"You must miss your wife and daughter."

"There isn't a day goes by I don't think of 'em. The other morning I was lyin' in my sleeping bag thinkin' of how we planned on maybe setting up a little bed and breakfast joint in the mountains somewhere. My thoughts started drifting and I got to thinkin' about an incident that happened years ago.

"I'd been on a four month hell-bent-for-leather drinking binge and thought it best I get a job back in the bush someplace where there wasn't booze around every corner. I ended up gettin' a job in a guiding camp in the foothills. One night I drove into town to pick up some supplies and ended up havin' a few drinks. By the time I was ready to head back I was feeling pretty good. I ended up lashing an old antique fire wagon to the back o' the truck, and away I went. The old wagon was zig-zaggin' down the highway behind me like a three legged jackrabbit. I was only a few miles out o' town when the Mounties pulled me over. I was charged with theft and drunken drivin'.

"Call it special providence or whatever you want to call it, but I had a lucky day. The judge gave me a choice – either I pay a three hundred and fifty dollar fine and do eighty hours community service work or spend six months in the can. I managed to round up enough money to pay the fine and ended up volunteering at the YMCA. I got to know a few o' the guys who worked there and we put together a little softball team for the young fellas on weekends. I had quite a bit o' time to do some serious thinking out in the fresh air, chasin' balls all over the place, and came to the conclusion that the only way I was going to get my life straightened out was to get involved in something that would keep me away from the juice.

"I got a job at a gas station. The mechanic in the garage was a pretty good guy and long story short I ended up gettin' my mechanic's license. There were times I thought I was going to go crazy if I didn't have a drink but I did a lot o' walkin' and worked at getting my mind focused on more positive things."

"Do you think you'll ever settle down again?"

"If it happens it happens, but if I die a single man I guess that's the way it goes."

"When did you say Nestor was going to be here?"

"He should be here any time now." He stood up and looked down the trail. "I'll be damned if I don't hear his truck comin' now."

In a few minutes Nestor pulled up beside Leonard's truck. He opened the passenger door. Leonard looked inside. "Holy crap. You got a new one."

"I couldn't get one from the wreckers. They said it would take too long."

Leonard went to the fire and poured two cups of coffee. They hunkered down beside the truck. Dayton unfolded a cot KhakiPants had given him and stretched out, pulling his cap over his eyes.

"How are the old boys doin'?"

"Pretty good. The one you call Grin is back now. I asked them if they wanted to come along for the ride but they said it was a good moon for fishing so they wanted to go out and catch a few walleyes."

"What does the moon have to do with fishing, anyway?" Dayton said. "You have to be nuts if you think the moon is going to decide if you catch fish or not."

"The moon is one of the most powerful forces in nature," Nestor said. "The moon itself isn't but its effect on Earth is evident in a lot of areas. It creates the tides, for one thing."

"You guys have powerful forces for everything, don't you?"

"No. We don't have powerful forces for everything. But nature is very close to us. It is part of us. White people look at the wilderness as being nice scenery. It isn't much deeper for them than that because they don't experience it the same way we do. They aren't as close to it as we are. Before we started turning into apple Indians – red on the outside and white on the inside – before we came to rely on the technology the white men brought us, we had learned how to balance our lives with nature and rely on it to provide us with what we needed. It has always been an important part of our lives and we have a lot of respect for it."

"Let's go for a stroll, Nestor. I've got something I want to show you."

They went to the edge of the clearing. Leonard put one of Dayton's empty pop cans into the pouch of a giant, two-tree slingshot. He pulled back hard and let go. The can careened recklessly through the air and landed short of the bam tree.

"That's quite a rig you've got there," Nestor said. "But I think you need a little more practice." They hunted down the pop can and sat in the shade. "How long do you think it will take to put the manifold in?"

"It's hard to say. It's quite a job if the bolts don't want to come out. You better give me a couple o' days, to be on the safe side. Today and tomorrow. It should be ready the day after tomorrow. When I get your truck done I'm gonna start cleanin' up the little house out back o' the gas station. I can run your truck out to the lake when I'm done with it, or you can come to the garage and trade trucks there. That might be a little easier for me, so I can concentrate on my house cleaning."

Nestor unbuttoned his shirt pocket. "I've got something here you might be interested in."

He dug out two toothpicks and handed them to Leonard. "We found them at your gravesite."

"These are the kind o' toothpicks KhakiPants always has."

"I'll bring you down some walleye fillets when I come for the truck."

"Sounds good. We can take the tamarack rails to Slave Lake whenever you're ready."

They returned to the trucks. Nestor pulled a large toolbox out of the back of his. "These are the tools Chap set out for you. And I just thought of something. If I bring you some walleye fillets, how are you going to cook them? There won't be any power or gas in the house."

"I'll borrow Dayton's propane camp stove the roadboys gave him."

Nestor got into Leonard's truck and headed out to the highway.

"I don't think Nestor was very polite, talking to me the way he did," Dayton pouted.

"It's obvious you don't understand a lot o' things about native culture. You seem to think it's a bunch o' mumbo jumbo, or whatever the term was KhakiPants used. When you make a comment like you did to Nestor you can expect he's probably gonna say something in return. It goes both ways, you know."

"And you're the expert, I suppose."

"I'm no expert but I have enough Indian blood in me that I respect the fact Nestor's entitled to believe what he wants to believe, the same as you and me."

"You're probably the only person I know, besides those guys, who gives a damn about native culture."

"The times are changin'. A lot o' people are more aware of native issues nowadays because it's becoming clearer for them to see that they've been swept under the rug too long. A lot of white Anglo Saxon Prodestants are beginning to see that the native community hasn't been treated very well, considering they signed treaties well over a hundred and fifty years ago and are still waiting for the government to honour the terms o' those treaties. A lot of aboriginal people are gettin' weary of waiting. They're not as interested in smokin' a peace pipe as they used to be. When they signed the treaties most of 'em didn't know what they were signin'. They weren't too big on English in those days.

"Things have changed considerably over the years, and one of these days First Nations people are gonna react in their own way if the government continues to persist in treating 'em like second class citizens. They've pretty well run out o' patience because of what's been happening and what hasn't been happening, and they're ready to react one way or another."

"What good is that going to do?"

"I think more people, natives *and* WASPs, are going to get activated. What's happening with Idle No More is a good example. And how about this? At Standing Rock in North Dakota there were close to a hundred and fifty tribes, many of whom had fought against each other in days past, who got together to peacefully protest a multi-billion dollar pipeline. While in the process of wantonly destroying sacred ground on native land the pipeline contractor had guard dogs attack several protestors. You didn't see much of it on mainstream news because there's a lot of oil money supporting television stations these days. But that gives you an idea of what the aboriginal community is prepared to do.

"And while I'm talking about it, how about this for news suppression? On dozens of reservations they haven't had clean drinking water for years. Some of them are rationed out bottled water that's supposed to hold them over for a month. But they never have enough. They have to keep clean and wash clothes and cook and all the rest of it. Some of 'em haven't had their own clean drinking water for twenty years. Shoal Lake First Nation 40 has been waiting for a century, if you can imagine, to have an accessible road built out to the highway because the city of Winnipeg expropriated thousands of acres of their land in order to divert drinking water from Shoal Lake to the townsfolk, cutting off their access to the highway in the process.

"This is the part that rattles me. The federal government has been telling First Nations for decades they're going to get to the bottom of the problem and they're going to get everything fixed up, like they said they were going to do if they won the election. They're going to build new schools for the kids and new homes for the residents and they're going to fix up the roads and put in proper bridges and all the rest of it, 'but not before we do the necessary research required to assist us in getting to the crux of the problem so we can implement the most suitable programs to get the job done as effectively and expeditiously as possible.' If that isn't another crock o' bureaucratic bullshit I don't know what it is. So like I was sayin' – given the appropriate set of circumstances I can see things starting to bust open any time now."

"That doesn't mean anything. Not to me, anyway."

"I'm not tryin' to pretend I know everything that's going on, 'cuz I don't. I'll give you my interpretation of the way I see things and you can make of it what you want. I look at the present situation with the native community as bein' similar to a dry spruce log sitting on a bed of hot coals. It's an analogy that's been growin' in my subconscious over the years. It changes a bit every time I think about it but it goes somethin' like this.

"A dry spruce log has to heat up to its kindling point before it will ignite. If there's enough heat under it, and it sits there long enough, it'll catch fire once it reaches its kindling point. When that happens, all the latent energy that's stored up inside comes to life, and *whomp!* – there's fire. The way I see it, the latent energy in the log is similar to the latent energy in the native community. It's there. It just hasn't reached its kindling point yet. But you can rest assured when things get hot enough a lot 'o people are going to get activated.

"Another way to look at it is that the bed of glowing coals the log's sitting in represents the heat of oppression the aboriginal community has been subjected to since the white man essentially stole their land from 'em. Sooner or later that oppression is going to reach its kindling point, and like a log on hot coals the energy that has been suppressed will be freed. I'm not very good at makin' up parables but that gives you an idea of how I'm seein' things."

"Yeah. I know. They're going to overtake the parliament buildings and all the white guys will be turned into slaves."

Leonard walked up to his face. "You don't even want to try to understand what's goin' on, do ya? You could care less."

"I could care *less* than less."

28

Leonard fastened the top button of his shirt, shoved his hands into his pockets and stood in front of the fire.

"You look cold."

"I am. And I'm a little confused. I didn't get much sleep last night."

"What time did you get in?"

"It was after two sometime. It took longer to haul the rails than we thought it would. We had to drive pretty slow, and we made two trips. But we had time to talk about a lot o' things, so it was a worthwhile trip all things considered. One interesting thing I found out was that Nestor's planning on goin' to university in the spring.

"On the way back I stopped in Valleyview to pick up a coffee for the road. They didn't have any 'to go' lids, so the waitress put a coffee filter over the top o' the cup and wrapped an elastic band around it. It didn't work the greatest but you have to give her credit for trying. It was pourin' like hell when I got back in the truck and when I got out on the highway I could hardly see the road in front o' me for the rain. There was coffee spilled all over my pants so I just cruised along, nice 'n easy.

"When I passed the roadcamp I noticed a Cat idling beside the office trailer. I thought it odd, a Cat idling in the pouring rain at that time o' day, so I parked the truck and turned off the lights. It wasn't long before Slick came out o' the office and crawled up onto the Cat. There was a big blue tarpaulin wrapped around something chained to the blade of the Cat. It was hard to tell what it was, bein' pitch dark with the rain pourin' down and the cab o' the truck full o' smoke, so I put on my raincoat and got out to take a closer look. I figured they might have busted up a piece of equipment and Slick was bringin' out a new part. I huddled behind a pile o' gas drums for a few minutes and away he went, down the new road.

"I was so tired I could've slept on a fencepost. Ya gotta work hard if you're gonna keep up with Nestor. I kept wonderin' what Slick was doing out there with a Cat in the middle of a blinding rainstorm in the middle o' the night and I think I only got two or three hours' sleep. What are you up to today?"

"Nothing. They said not to bother showing up until the rain stops. What time is it?"

Leonard dug the watch out of his watch pocket. "Nine thirty. It's gonna rain all day by the looks of it. I'm gonna see if I can grab a couple more hours sleep. I think I might go for a hike later on."

"You're nuts. You're going to end up getting sick."

"I don't get sick. Sick is a word that isn't in my vocabulary."

"It doesn't matter if it's in your vocabulary or not. You're going to get so run down you won't be able to get out of bed."

"I don't think about it so I don't give it a chance to happen." He pulled out his tobacco. "Besides, I discovered a cure years ago."

"What do you mean – you discovered a cure?"

"My old man was a trucker. I think I might've already told you that. He probably ate in every roadhouse café between Winnipeg and Halifax. When I was in my early teens I went out on a few runs with him. On one trip we were on I had a stomach ache from something I'd eaten earlier. It was about then I got to thinking maybe the reason the old man never got sick was because over the years, in all the greasy spoon joints he had eaten in, he probably picked up the odd bug here and there and as he gradually loaded more bugs into his system his immunity built up to the point where he could eat almost anything without havin' to suffer the consequences of a less-than-satisfactory meal.

"I knew I wasn't gonna be a trucker, eatin' at roadside cafés all the time, so I got to wondering how I could get some bugs into my own system. I more or less forgot about it until one day when I was readin' an interesting article in the paper about how the Mafia owned legitimate-lookin' businesses strictly for the purpose o' laundering dirty money. And there it was – right in front o' my eyes. *Dirty money*. And I had a bunch of it sittin' in the watch pocket of my jeans. I dug out a penny and stuck it in my mouth and started suckin' on it, but it didn't take long before I began seein' dark images o' some of the places the hands that touched that penny might've been. I spat it out and started givin' my newfound theory some serious rethink. I decided it would probably be sufficient if I just licked a penny once a day to get some good germs from who-knows-where into my system."

"You're kidding."

"Nope. I did it for a few months, off and on, until I realized it wasn't the smartest thing in the world to do. But I ain't dead yet. In fact I feel pretty good, all things considered. I haven't had a cold or the flu in years."

"I suppose you want to go out there to see what he was doing with the Cat."

"I think I might. You should join me."

"No way. Nobody in his right mind would go out there on a day like today. I think I'm going to go to Valleyview and do some laundry and check up on the trailer. If it quits raining I might go out to the beaver pond tomorrow, but that's as far as I'm going."

29

Thunder penetrated thick air. Leonard nestled a log into the fire. Dayton pulled a burnt sausage off a stick and dropped it onto a plate of beans.

"You should come to the pit with me," Leonard said. "We've got the whole day ahead of us."

"Have you got any more spinners? Mine must of fallen out of my pack on the trail somewhere."

Leonard dug through his fishing bag. "These are the ones I've been usin'." He tossed a small plastic box to Dayton. "How about it? It's less than an hour's walk from here."

"I'm not going to the borrow pit. I told you that yesterday. I said I was going as far as the beaver pond. I'm staying here."

Leonard buttoned up his jacket. "Suit yourself." He grabbed a tamarack rail he had been using as a walking stick and headed into the bush.

It started sprinkling. Digging a horse blanket out of the lean-to, Dayton draped it over his shoulders, pulled his cap over his eyes and went to sleep. Several hours later Leonard's clamoring down the trail awakened him.

"You make a lot of noise. I was trying to sleep."

Leonard combed his hair back with his hands. "Bears. That's why I was makin' so much noise. I wanted to let 'em know I wasn't interested in visiting. I'm gonna have to change into some dry clothes. I think it's going to be a little nasty tomorrow too, by the looks o' things."

"Was it worth coming all the way out here just so you could walk around in the muck at the borrow pit?"

"I figured Slick was up to something the other night."

"What did he do?"

"I don't know for sure, but he must have been out all night. There's a mound o' mud pushed up where the spur road enters the borrow pit clearing. He made two trips with the Cat. I'm willing to bet he brought those pod contrivances out here."

"You said he made two trips. What would he make two trips for?"

"When I was watchin' him at the roadcamp I could see something wrapped in a tarpaulin, chained to the blade o' the Cat. I think that was the first pod he took out. It was probably too awkward for him to load up the second one by himself so he had to make two trips."

"You don't even know what the pods look like. You can't say for sure that that's what it was."

"All I know is there's a mound o' mud over there and I'd be willing to bet my last dollar there are two cement pods under it."

"Like I told you guys at the lake – as far as I'm concerned Kawatina doesn't exist, no matter *what* you found over there. You wanted to see what was out there and you did, so are you going to leave this alone now?"

"Nope. I wanna know for sure if they *are* the pods. And if they are, I want to know why he brought 'em out in the middle o' the night in the pourin' rain instead o' when they dug the pit, like they said they were gonna do."

"They said they were going to put the bodies in the pods and that's probably what they did. Maybe they weren't built yet when they dug the pit so they shoved the bodies into the corner until they were ready."

"The guy with the fancy suit said they were already built. And here's another thing. I reburied the bodies but somehow they knew I reburied 'em 'cuz they came in and dug 'em up again. *They* didn't dig 'em up. KhakiPants did."

"He couldn't of. He took a couple of days off. When I stopped in at the roadcamp to drop off the paperwork I got from the Edmonton office the cook told me he was in Calgary for a few days. So he couldn't of been the one that dug up the graves."

"Nestor found a bunch o' toothpicks – the kind he's always chewin' on – at my gravesite. I know for a fact Slick wouldn't go anywhere near a set o' human bones if his life depended on it. No matter what the camp cook told ya, your buddy KhakiPants was the one who dug up my graves, whether he wants to admit it or not."

"The main thing is that the bodies are in the pods now. They'll probably wait until it dries out and then they'll bury them properly."

"I don't think that's gonna happen. I don't think the bodies are even *in* the pods."

"Where would they be, then?"

"I think the reason Slick brought the pods out was because the operation's shut down for the rain, and none o' the road crew is in camp now. He knew it would be a good time to get 'em out here without anybody seein' anything. This could end up bein' bad news with Forestry if they find out native graves had been dug up. KhakiPants probably told him to get the pods out here in case Forestry comes lookin' for graves they had no knowledge of previously. That way they can cover their butts. They'll say they accidently dug up a couple of overgrown Indian graves and knew they had to rebury 'em properly."

"You're saying they went through all the trouble of bringing the pods out here just so they'll look good in Forestry's eyes if they find out about the graves."

"Yup."

"It doesn't make any sense to me to go through all the trouble of bringing the pods out here, if that's actually what he did, and then not put the bodies in them."

"The night we got back from showin' KhakiPants the graves, when we were all sittin' around the stewpot, he said Slick could have come out to look at 'em but had no desire to go anywhere near dead bodies. He used the excuse he had some welding to do and had to stay in camp. So keepin' that in mind, pushin' the bodies into a brush pile with a Cat is probably about as close as Slick's ever gonna get to 'em. The only reason he pushed 'em into a pile in the first place was because KhakiPants probably told him to. There's no way I can see him puttin' the bodies, bone by bone, into the pods."

"But that's what they're for."

"Now that they've dug up the bodies again, after I re-buried 'em, I wouldn't be surprised if they burn the bones up later on sometime. That way they'll know Forestry can't get 'em for disturbing a grave 'cuz there'll be nothin' left. Like I was saying, the only reason the pods are over there now is for insurance – in case Forestry learns about the graves while they're still workin' on the road. I'll tell ya what. Why don't we settle this once and for all. We can talk 'til the cows come home about pods 'n bones 'n everything under the sun but the only way we're gonna know what's over there is to get a shovel and start diggin."

"Oh no you don't."

"I'll do the diggin'. If the pods are buried under the muck I'll bust 'em open and we can see what's inside. If the bodies are in 'em I won't make another peep, and I'll leave this whole thing alone."

"What if the bodies aren't in them?"

"We don't know for sure if it's pods *buried* out there. The first thing to do is see what we can find with the shovel."

"And you'll forget about this altogether if the bodies are in the pods?"

"Yup."

"And you'll do the digging?"

"Yup."

"This is the last time I'm going over there."

They gathered their things and headed out. The rain started coming down in sheets. A blue wind howled out of the north. It was a long hour before they reached the road.

"What's up there?" Dayton said.

"The road into the borrow pit. It won't take long now."

They slopped down the spur road and huddled under a spruce tree beside a mound of mud. Leonard pulled a plastic bag over his head.

"Why are you so interested in Kawatina?" Dayton said.

"It's personal, I guess. I have enough Indian in me that I like to know what's goin' on with some o' the stuff I hear about."

"I'm freezing," Dayton said. "A shot of rum would hit the spot right now. But you don't drink anymore."

"Nope. I quit drinkin' when I got my mechanic's license. I've always been a bit of a reader and I started readin' about the power of the mind – about how we can change certain things in our lives if we concentrate on replacing negative thoughts with positive ones." He stood up into a boughful of rainwater, the plastic bag over his eyes, and pulled out his wallet. "When I was fightin' my alcoholism I came up with a little slogan. I've been usin' it for years. It gives me a boost when things start gettin' a little tough." He handed Dayton a small, homemade card.

Every step I take is one less step I have to make.

"You wrote that?"

"Yup. And it works. It gets stronger the more you use it. I was lucky because those words came to me at a time when I needed 'em most. It took a while, but they got me past my addiction to booze. And now they get me through a lot of other things."

Dayton handed back the card and looked over at the greasy mound. "You're still serious about digging up that pile of crap? There must be six feet of muck there."

"I'll dig all day if I have to." Leonard opened his packsack and pulled out a large coffee can.

"Is that what I think it is?"

Leonard shook the can. "It's what I had stashed at the woodpile. I figured the right thing to do would be to put it back where it belongs. I can't connect it to the rest of her 'cuz I don't know where the rest of her is, so I'll bury it here where it belongs." He got up and, tucking the can under his arm, grabbed the shovel. "I'll bury it in the borrow pit. I'll start diggin' up the mound when I get back."

It was two hours before the shovel blade thunked against a hard object buried in the mud. Leonard got the axe and took several heavy swings at an exposed piece of cement. He reached into the opening he had created and pulled out a handful of straw. He filled his cup with thermos coffee, ate a cold pancake and belched. Dayton woke up and looked around, filled with sleep. Leonard tossed the straw toward him.

"What's that?" Dayton rasped.

"The bodies I was diggin' for."

"Where did you get that from?"

Leonard pointed with his thumb to the mud pile.

Dayton went to the mound.

"Go ahead," Leonard said. "Stick your hand in there. It isn't gonna bite."

Dayton pulled out more straw. "How come they said they were going to put the bodies in the pods?"

"The graves were in their way so they mowed 'em under. Slick came back here with a Cat and stuck these things in the ground so it would look like they had moved the bodies, like I was tellin' ya."

"Now what?"

Leonard started refilling the hole, tamping down the wet, heavy clay. "I want to talk to Nestor about this. I think he'd be interested in seein' what they've done. Then I'm gonna have another chat with those goofballs at the roadcamp."

30

Leonard bolted into the office trailer. Slick, sitting at the table, didn't look up from his paperwork.

"You've got some explaining to do," Leonard said.

Slick put a calculator into the filing cabinet, locked it and left the office. He got into his truck and drove out onto the highway.

Leonard grabbed a felt marker from the table and stuffed it into his jacket pocket.

Slick was cleaning the mud off his boots with a screwdriver when Leonard pulled into camp. "This isn't very good fishing weather, is it?" he said.

Leonard dug a chunk of cement out of his pocket and held it toward him. "I busted this off the pods."

"I wondered how they made them things." Slick pulled a handful of photographs out of the cab of his truck. "These ones turned out pretty good. I like the one where you're stuffing straw into a pod. That's probably one of the best ones."

"Where did these come from?"

"What's our business is our business."

"The straw was already in the pods. Where the bodies were supposed to be."

"I think it's some kind of criminal offense to be playing around with the dead like that. I thought you would have had a little more respect. Where'd you put them?"

"Where did I put what?"

"The bodies. Where did you put the bodies?"

Leonard re-examined the photo showing him with a handful of straw. "I'm pullin' straw *out* o' the pod, not puttin' it in."

"I can't be so sure about that. To me it looks like you're putting straw *in*. One thing I know for sure is that you trespassed on a private road easement, and to top it off you dug up the pods and stole the bodies and stuffed the pods full of straw."

"Nestor and Allan are out there now. They're gonna turn over every rock in the country 'til they find the bodies. They've already found some toothpicks. The kind your buddy with the baggy pants chews on all the time. I went out to the lake to see 'em when I got back from diggin' up the pods. I wanted 'em to know what you yahoos did out there."

"I hear that the weather has been pretty nice down south in stubble country. Why don't you go back where you came from, where you won't get into any trouble." Slick got into his truck and opened the window. "If you hit the road I'll forget I saw these photographs. We can build our road and you can jump some stubble and everybody'll be happy." He turned the truck around and drove out to the highway.

"You better forget about this grave bullshit before we both end up in jail," Dayton said.

"They set it up. That's why Slick took the pods out there. He wanted to be sure they were buried at the borrow pit so they could have this whole thing set up. And I'll tell ya something else.

I don't think Muskeg Marty's a camper. I'd be willin' to bet he's some kind o' photographer. His packsack's probably full of cameras and special lenses so he can get good shots from a long ways away. I wouldn't be surprised if it was his job to keep his eye on things. He's the only person who could have taken those pictures.

"This is the way I see it. KhakiPants went out to see the graves so he could see firsthand what the lay o' the land was. From what their surveyors had reported they knew the graveyard area was the only place they could get the dirt they needed to plug up the muskeg. They had to set it up so they could cover their asses if necessary. I'm thinkin' that somewhere along the line you mentioned to 'em I was planning on goin' down to get my truck. They knew it would take a couple o' days for that to transpire because I'd be hundreds o' miles away. But they had to come up with a way to get you out o' here at the same time so they could do their thing without havin' to worry about either one of us wanderin' over to the gravesite area."

"They needed the power plant so they could set up lights for the night shift," Dayton said. "They have to take advantage of the good weather while they can."

"To my way o' thinkin' they could've picked up the power plant most any time. Slick's had lots o' time on his hands lately. They got both of us headed down to

Whitecourt with the idea I'd help ya load the light plant onto your truck, although a diesel power plant probably weighs about as much as an empty submarine. I was planning on getting my truck anyway so I didn't have a problem goin' down there with ya. When you phoned Slick from the gas station to tell him we were headed for Whitecourt he probably had a bulldozer fired up and headed over to the gravesite within an hour. You ended up sittin' around in Whitecourt waiting for them to phone ya about the power plant that never did show up, and to be sure you wouldn't be around here anywhere they turned around and sent ya to Edmonton to pick up some paperwork.

"They said they had the pods specially built. That way we'd be under the impression they were tryin' to cooperate. But their actual plan was to remove every indication of there ever *bein'* any graves out there. I showed up, discovered what they had done and dug two new graves. Somehow or other they knew about my graves and they dug *them* up. Then Slick takes the pods out in the middle o' the night and buries 'em along the edge o' the clearing.

"Now they know their butts are gonna be covered if we should happen to mention anything to Forestry about there bein' native graves out there. And to top it off they have pictures of me breakin' into the pods. If Forestry doesn't find out they dug up the graves by the time they get the road built they aren't gonna say anything to anybody 'cuz they'll have eliminated the graves and nobody's gonna know any different 'cuz they've got all the bases covered. On top o' that they've offered you a cushy job so they know you aren't gonna say anything."

"I happened to be in the right place at the right time, and I'm ready to do whatever it takes to get on board."

Leonard dug the watch out of his jeans. "I'm gonna run over to the gas station. I wanna talk to Chap about movin' the house. If Nestor and Allan show up they can catch me there or wait here. I shouldn't be more 'n an hour."

31

"What time was it when Nestor left last night?"

"I'm not sure, but it was pretty late. We had a lot to talk about. They couldn't believe what they saw out there. The roadboys pushed the brush pile into the borrow pit and set it on fire. The way Nestor was talkin' you'd never know by the looks o' things now that there were ever any graves out there atall. Allan was livid. When they got back here he kept walkin' out to the highway. He said he was gonna get Slick's pelt. Nestor said he's never seen him act that way. I told him I'd approach Slick and KhakiPants and threaten to get Forestry involved, but like he said – they'll deny knowin' anything about Kawatina because they've effectively wiped it out. I'm gonna have to go out there and take a look."

"All they did was burn the brush pile."

"I want to see what they did."

"I'm going to have a nap."

It was late afternoon when Leonard reached the borrow pit. The brush pile had been burned, as Nestor had said. They didn't miss a stick. Soft, grey ashes covered the bottom of the pit. All that remained was a small gas drum on the edge of the clearing. Leonard unscrewed the bung on the barrel, rolled it to the bottom of the pit and dropped a match on the trail of gasoline.

He went back to the beaver pond and built a small fire. Rain started smattering against the tarpaulin lean-to. He crawled under it, gathered up thick moss piled in a corner and formed it into a mattress. After smoking a cigarette he went to sleep.

He awakened at four thirty in the morning. The rain had stopped. It was time to get moving.

Dayton was gone when he reached camp. A note had been left under the tent flap. He was to get to the roadcamp right away.

He parked beside KahkiPants's truck and went into the office trailer. It was empty. Slipping in greasy mud he went to the kitchen trailer. KhakiPants and the cook were sitting at a table. KhakiPants stood up when he opened the door.

"What's up? Dayton left me a note."

"I'm afraid I have some unfortunate news. Your native friend – the younger fella – was in some kind of accident out on the highway. He's in the hospital in Peace River."

"What happened?"

"We don't know, but it sounds like he's in pretty bad shape."

"This happened out on the highway, you say."

"Just out here. On the other side of the hill."

"I gotta get goin'."

Dayton was waiting for him at the front door of the hospital.

"There's no point going in. He's gone."

"What happened?"

"He was in the ditch. That's all they told me."

"Where's Nestor and the old boys?"

"I went out to the lake to tell them. They were here for a while. Nestor said they'd be at camp. There's no point staying here."

Nestor and the old boys were huddled under a tarpaulin when they got back to camp. Leonard hadn't spoken since leaving the hospital.

"I'm goin' for a walk."

"It's pouring rain."

"There's a raincoat around here someplace."

He went into the tent. Nestor followed.

"There's nothing you could have done, Leonard."

Leonard slouched onto his sleeping bag. Nestor sat cross-legged in front of him. "Allan liked you. He told me you were his friend. He said he trusted you. He wanted you to know that but he didn't see you very often and didn't talk to you very much. I've got something for you." He jammed his hand into his shirt pocket and pulled out a jackknife. "Allan had a lot of respect for you. He told me he was going to give it to you some day. It's his carving knife."

"When's the funeral?"

"I'm not sure. I have to make the arrangements."

32

Leonard parked the truck in the ditch and started walking down the long hill into Peace River. It was five in the morning. Cold, wet wind washed the highway. Rain clung to his clothes like honey. He huddled under a train bridge at the bottom of the hill and opened his knapsack. Digging out a coffee can, he placed his hands on the lid while a train rumbled silently above him.

He walked over to the bus station. A tired young woman, slouched in a plastic chair, rocked a baby carriage. Coffee from a dented brown metal machine came out in rude, brown spurts. He went to the window. Water had filled the low spots in the street. A gust of wind wrapped a sheet of rain around a wobbling streetlight.

Several blocks away, sitting on the curb across the street from the RCMP detachment, he unscrewed the cup from his thermos, spilling coffee on his leg, his leg now the only warm thing, while the dark town around him slept. He held the coffee can up at arm's length and shouted.

"Watina!"

33

Wind stirred long grass. Leonard leaned against a rail fence and adjusted the tie at his throat. A rented black suit, a crumpled sail, hung awkwardly from his shoulders.

Six people had attended the funeral: Nestor, himself, the old boys, a priest and an elderly native woman. It was quiet and honourable.

Allan was only twenty seven years old. There were so many young graves. Thunder filled the grey afternoon. He leaned on the rail in the rain, his hair clinging to the shoulders of the suit, his pants sticking to his legs. *If only the rain would put out all the fires.*

He slopped to the truck and pulled a large willow cross and an axe out of the box. Chopping a hole in the ground, he planted the cross and closed his eyes, kneeling.

Lightning sharpened the sky. He returned to the truck, dragging the axe behind him.

34

It was a long hike to Kawatina although he knew every turn in the trail, every fallen log, every small clear creek. Walking became arduous, his not having eaten for two days.

He stopped at the beaver pond and cupped his hands in the blue spring. Rivers of cold water rolled off his cleanly-shaven face.

It would have been Lyla's birthday today. She would have been thirteen. A teenager. He had always made his own birthday card for her. She had saved them all. She felt silly wearing braces. Her teeth would straighten out and she'd be even prettier, her mother had assured her. Maureen helped her with her homework. Showed her how to make oatmeal cookies. She was a wonderful mother and Lyla such a wonderful child. He looked toward the hill where another mother and daughter had spent time together. They had been resting side by side, as were Maureen and Lyla.

He knelt on the sodden ground, the sky above him and the world around him a blur. Picking himself up, he continued walking. His energy all but spent when he reached the base of the hill, he grasped a tree branch along the edge of the trail and pulled. *Every step I take…is one less step…Ihavetomake.*

Reaching the crest of the hill, he sat across from Grin, hunched at a small fire. Short, grey whiskers dotted his chin.

A feeling of repose stirred his thoughts, and he recognized that nothing was unfair. Nothing required justification. Everything simply existed. Everything simply *was*.

35

"You've been quiet this morning, Leonard. I'm sorry to hear what happened to your native friend. Have you been doing anything with the house?"

Leonard looked up from the morning newspaper.

"How are you were making out with the house?"

"Pretty good. It's in pretty good shape."

"My father built it. He was a stickler for doing things right."

"I peeled back some o' the planks to get an idea of what it would take to get it off the foundation. I'd be interested in buyin' it if you'd be interested in sellin' it."

"What would you do with it?"

"I'm beginnin' to like it a bit around here. I thought it might be a good idea to buy an acre or two of bushed land. The little house would probably feel comfortable enough sittin' in a place like that."

"Haha. I suppose it would, all right. I know a realtor in Valleyview. He might have an idea where there are a few acres for sale. I'll call him tonight." Chap refilled Leonard's cup. "I feel a little awkward having to tell you this, especially now that you say you'd like to buy the house, but I'm afraid I'm going to have to withdraw the job offer I gave you."

"What's up?"

"I told you that the mechanic I had before had stomach surgery. The doctors told him he'd have to find some kind of work that wouldn't involve any heavy lifting. He dropped in a few days ago. He looked better than he has in years. He'd like to get back into the shop again if there's any way he can avoid the heavy work. I told him I had approached you about working here and he asked me what I thought of the idea of having him do the tune ups and oil changes and whatnot if you'd be willing to do the jobs requiring muscle work."

"It wouldn't be full time, then."

"No. Just when we'd need you. Sorry about giving you the runaround like this but he's an old friend and he knows everyone in the country. He's brought a lot of work to the shop."

"I guess that would be all right. Maybe I can pick up a little extra work on the side."

"You're still welcome to use the house, though. We decided to wait until spring before we put the new one up. If you're still interested in getting an acreage I'll see if I can find out what might be available."

"Sounds good."

"You must have some French in you. Your last name's duSace."

"I do, as a matter o' fact. I've got a good shot of Mohawk and a dab of courier de bois in my blood."

"A fella stopped in yesterday and asked if I could put a new transmission in his grain truck. Would you be interested in doing that? It would give you a bit of a start in the shop, to give you a feel for things."

"When does he want to get it done?"

"Not for a few days yet."

"That should work out all right. Once I'm livin' in the house it'll be easier to get in touch with me me when something comes up. You wouldn't have a couple o' lanterns kickin' around, would you? It wouldn't hurt to brighten things up a bit in there."

"I think there's a coal oil lamp in the cellar. If not I'll order a couple and they should be here in two or three days."

"You better get naptha lamps. They're a lot brighter." Leonard headed for the door. "Looks like you've got somebody sittin' at the gas pumps."

36

"What time does the gas station close?"

"Ten. No. Seven. Seven o'clock on Sundays."

"It's almost seven thirty. Do you think I can still pick up some propane? They need some for one of the operator's campers."

"Chap's a good guy. If he's still there he'll help you out."

Dayton was out of camp in a minute.

Leonard was splitting fire logs when Nestor's truck broke the silence. Leonard walked down the trail and met up with him.

They lowered the tailgate and sat on it.

Nestor shook his head before speaking. "The guys on the road crew. The foreman and the Super. I can't figure them out. It seems like if it isn't one thing, it's another."

"What are they up to now?"

"They came out to the lake. I couldn't understand what in the world they'd be coming out to see us for."

Leonard waited for more. It was slow in coming.

"The way Slick was talking, once they get the bridge put across the river they're going to call it the Kawatina bridge. He said they want to show their respect by naming the bridge after it. But it's none of their business. Kawatina is none of their business. It isn't anybody else's business, either. Before Allan started going out there it didn't have a name. Everyone knew what it was without it having to have a name. If word gets out there's a sacred native burial ground around here you can be sure people will come out on the new road in their four wheel drives with shovels in the back. The roadboys say they're doing it out of respect for Kawatina but to us it looks more like they're doing it to shove it in our faces. If they had the respect for it they say they have they would have left it alone. Stan…Grin has been slipping a little lately. He was upset when they dug up the graves, and then we lost Allan. He's an old man. He can't take it as well as we can. He's resting now but I think this is getting to be a bit too much for him."

"We can't resurrect the gravesite, and we can't get Allan back, but we can talk to those morons about the bridge. We better run up to the roadcamp and have a chat with 'em."

"They said they were going to Peace River after they talked to me. One of the bigshots from Edmonton is supposed to be there. The way they were talking I think it might be the guy who was here before. The guy who always wears a fancy suit."

"We can be there first thing in the morning."

"I'd like to, but I should stay in camp."

"Sure. I'll go myself. I'll see if I can find something for Grin when I'm in town."

Dayton's truck was approaching. Nestor slid off the tailgate. "I better be getting back. If you don't mind stopping in tomorrow I'd like to know how your visit went." He backed his truck into the trees. Dayton passed.

Leonard went back to the fire and sat on the splitting block. Dayton fidgeted with the license plate of his truck. "Do you have your jackknife?"

Leonard tossed it to him. He loosened a screw on the license plate.

"That's a carving knife, not a screwdriver." Leonard dug a dime out of his watch pocket and loosened two screws. "Have ya quit drivin?"

"I sold the other truck to a guy on the road crew. I have to put a license plate on it so I can take it to the roadcamp. What does Nestor have to say these days?"

"KhakiPants went out to the lake with Slick. They wanted to talk to the guys. When they get a bridge across the river they want to call it the Kawatina bridge."

"What's wrong with that?"

"Kawatina has nothin' to do with them. I don't even know why they have to name it in the first place. It's only a bridge."

"You're getting worked up about it again and it's got nothing to do with you."

"It has more to do with me than it does with KhakiPants. I can tell ya that much."

"There's a lot of pressure on him to get the road finished. I was beginning to think that with all the lousy weather we've been getting, holding up construction on the road, and with all the stress he's been under from you guys about the graves, it wouldn't be worth having a job like he has that might end up giving him a heart attack or something. But one day when we were having coffee he said that he was looking forward to getting a comfortable pension. The way he was talking, when he retires he's going to be a fat cat. That's one of the reasons why I'm going to do whatever it takes to get on with these guys. If I end up with a pension like what he's talking about I don't have a problem doing whatever they want me to do.

"I might be going to Edmonton next week to the laser logger demonstration I told you about. They're getting it set up in an empty hangar at the old Municipal airport. There's only going to be a few company reps there because they want to keep it low key. They might not get everything put together as fast as they want to so they told me I might have to wait a little longer before they give me the go-ahead. What about your mechanicing job? You haven't been working too much in the shop."

"It's been a little slow because I'm only doin' the heavy duty jobs. The other mechanic, the fella who worked there before, seems to be keepin' fairly busy but I told Chap I wouldn't put my coveralls on unless a job comes in that the other mechanic won't be able to handle. Nestor's goin' to university in the spring. He asked me if I'd be interested in going to the city with him when he gets a few of his courses lined up. He hasn't done much drivin' in the city and he needs a navigator."

"You should come down with me when I go to the demonstration. You can check out the laser logger."

"I thought you said it was an exclusive demonstration. Just the company bigshots."

"They want to be careful who sees it. I'm working for them now in a way, so I don't think there would be a problem if you came along with me."

"I think I'll be happy enough stayin' where I am. Bring back some brochures or test results or something and I'll take a look at 'em. I might see ya in the mornin' and I might not. I'm going to talk to your buddies about the bridge."

"I think you'll be wasting your time. They'll be getting everything ready for the demonstration. They said they might be moving some stuff into my trailer. It sounds like it'll be ready for me to move into any day now."

Leonard was at a motel in Peace River at nine o'clock the following morning. Jogging up the stairs, he took a few deep breaths, stopped at the door and knocked.

KhakiPants answered. "Well. Who do we have here?"

Slick and The Suit were seated at a table. Slick went to the door. "We're not taking visitors today."

The Suit came to the door. "What's on your mind?"

"You guys."

"What are you spouting off about now?" Slick snorted. Leonard smelled booze on his breath.

"We don't need a commotion out here," The Suit said. "You've got five minutes."

"Nestor was out to see me last night. He said you went to see him at the lake."

"Why would that be any concern of yours?" Slick said.

"Nestor and his friends don't feel comfortable talkin' to you guys for some reason so I told 'em I'd be their spokesman. They're wonderin' why you want to call the bridge the Kawatina bridge. Apparently you didn't give 'em much of an explanation."

"It's none of your business what we call the bridge," Slick snapped. "If they want an explanation they can ask us for it. We thought we made a good choice. And we sure as hell don't need their approval. You didn't even know those guys before you came up here. I can tell you this much. You didn't stop us from getting to the gravesite and you didn't get us shut down for digging up the graves.   You didn't do much of anything when you get right down to it.   As far as I'm concerned, you're another half-breed drifter who isn't worth five cents.   The owner of the gas station told me where you come from.   That's where *all* you eastern half-breed bastards come from isn't it?"

Leonard's fist filled the foreman's face. He kneeled over, holding his hand against a bleeding nose.

KhakiPants started to say something. Leonard pushed him against the wall and grabbed his shirt collar with both hands. "I've had it with you goofballs."

37

A myriad of tangled thoughts ran through Leonard's mind as he sat in the canoe. He was angry with himself for having reacted the way he did at the motel. He paddled to shore and started a fire.

The droning of an outboard motor pierced the silence. In a few minutes an aluminum boat approached. It slowed and stopped at the shoreline. Grin, clutching a small plastic pail, climbed out. He gave the pail to Leonard.

They sat quietly at the fire, taking turns raking up small handfuls of Saskatoon berries. Leonard crawled into his pup tent and emerged with a large blue handkerchief, the four corners tied together. He extended it to the old boy.

Grin stuffed it under his shirt, climbed into the boat and pushed off. He headed back across the lake toward his tent, a dot of brown in the distance.

Leonard's thoughts thickened again. Maybe he needed a break. Maybe it would be best if he got on with other things. He could go back east. He could look for his brother. Maybe start up a little motorcycle shop. Maybe push Kawatina into a far recess of his mind and get on with life. He was disappointed with himself. He shouldn't have lost it the way he did. But Slick had pushed it too far.

38

Dayton's trailer smelled musty, as if sweaty laundry had been lingering in a damp corner too long. Leonard pulled a chair out from the kitchen table, snagging an upturned piece of linoleum.

"I just busted off a piece o' linoleum."

Dayton was making coffee. "Don't worry about it. They're almost at the river now so they're concentrating on getting everything set up properly to get the bridge put in. They said they'd get everything fixed up when they had the time."

"I'm goin' outside for a smoke." Leonard grabbed the door with both hands and pulled it open. "The door needs fixin', too. Two o' the hinges are busted off." He rolled a smoke and stood in front of a weatherworn trailer. Lengths of tin siding, long detached from smudgy rivets, hung awkwardly like thin, curled cardboard. The bedroom window was cracked and bandaged with pale masking tape. A piece of warped plywood covered the bathroom window.

Dayton came out with coffee and sat on the steps. "It's a little battered up now but it'll look a lot better when the repair guys get finished with it. I think they want me bad enough that they're giving me this stuff to make sure I don't jump ship."

Leonard stretched out on a pale, lumpy lawn and slurped his coffee. "Are ya sure you're gonna be dry in there?"

"I'm not worried about it. They're going to let me know any day now when the laser logger demonstration's going to be. I wouldn't be surprised if I'm in the Edmonton office pretty soon."

"Seems like a waste o' time fixin' this place up if they're gonna send ya to Edmonton."

"Maybe they're going to fix it up and give it to me as a bonus. I've been helping them out quite a bit. I could probably sell it. Do you want to buy it?"

"I'm thinkin' o' buyin' Chap's little house. I can probably get it for a decent price in view o' the fact he wants to get rid of it. It looks like you're doin' pretty good with this outfit. I don't imagine ya had to shell out too much for the truck, and your cellular phone must be worth a few bucks. You've even got yourself a real live Detroiter trailer. They've got your ass buttered so slick you could slide through a gravel pit."

"The stuff they're giving me has either been laying around or they haven't got any more use for it."

"I'm not so sure about that. The truck wasn't lyin' around. The cell phone wasn't, either. It looks like the trailer might have been sittin' in cobwebs for a while, though."

"I don't know how much you know about business but I can tell you this much. You have to take advantage of every opportunity you get. If they want to give me this stuff as a tradeoff because they want me to keep quiet about the graves, I don't have a problem with that. I'll take everything that comes my way."

"Getting a little greedy, aren't we?"

"I'm going to milk these guys for everything I can get. You can call it buttering my ass but I call it making the right moves."

"What about the guys at the lake? You've been talking down to 'em a lot."

"You start beaking off about the stuff they've given me and now you're trying to tell me how to talk to people. Everybody's different. You should mind your own business."

"The graves *are* my business. I made 'em my business. Those guys are my friends. I told Allan I wouldn't get Forestry involved in this because he was afraid if word got out a sacred burial ground had been discovered the hill would end up crammed with people with shovels jammed in the trunks o' their cars."

"The roadcrew obviously hasn't done anything wrong. I haven't seen the Great Spirit throw any fireballs at them."

"You don't want to be talking like that. It shows your ignorance."

"Do you call this ignorance? It looks like I'm the only one getting ahead around here."

"What about the way Slick and KhakiPants have been talkin' to the guys? They don't know the first thing about respect."

"The Indians don't even understand English. Not the old guys, anyway. All they're interested in doing is going out in their boat, or sitting at their fire staring at the clouds all day."

"I'm gonna help myself to one more cup o' coffee and then I have to be going." Leonard went inside.

Dayton came in a few minutes later. "I was just thinking about what you said about getting my ass buttered. Now that they're starting to show me their appreciation your reaction is to be defensive and tell me that they're buttering my ass. You think you're better than I am because now you're working at the garage and you're going to buy that house, and all I've got is an old Detroiter trailer."

"You better sit down. I think you're hyperventilating."

"Tonight you'll be freezing your balls off in your tent and I'll be watching TV, having a beer."

Leonard stood nose to nose with him. He lowered his voice. "The only thing you care about is yourself. You don't give a damn about the sacred ground or the graves or the guys any more than ya give a flyin' fuck about anything else. You didn't even have the decency go to Allan's funeral." Leonard yanked the door open, pulling the top hinge out of its mooring. "You're crap. You and the whole works of 'em!"

39

"Mornin', Chap. Looks like summer decided to wait until October this year."

Chap poured a coffee for Leonard and refilled his.

"What do you have here?" Leonard said, noting a blueprint lying on the counter.

"I'm going to put a little addition on. My daughter works in a convenience store in Grande Prairie. They make as much selling coffee and sandwiches as they do everything else. The wife and I were out to visit her last week. She showed me the till receipts for the day and I couldn't believe it. We talked about it when we got back to her place. She drew a sketch of how I could modify the gas station and put a little addition on it and set it up for different kinds of coffee and sandwiches. We've had a few summers where we kept open long after our normal quitting time, when the weather was good. You have to make money when you can in this business. Blaine – my daughter – thinks we should set up a coffee bar in here, and have ice cream cones in the summer. After seeing the till receipts at the end of her work day I think she might be right."

"So ya got yourself a blueprint made up."

"She did. It came on the bus last night. She wanted to surprise us."

Leonard studied the blueprint. "I know this much. Somebody around here must be makin' a killing off Dayton alone. He's always chompin' on something."

"He was in earlier on. He asked if I knew where you were."

The phone rang.

"Keep your eye on the gas pumps for me, would you?"

Leonard went out to the shop. He found an empty ice cream pail, filled it with water and started washing the large front window.

Dayton's truck pulled up beside him. The window opened. "I'm not very impressed with the way you were talking to me at the trailer. I think you owe me an apology."

"I've been thinkin' about it, and you're right. I had no business sayin' the things I did."

"I know that those guys are your friends but you don't have to go half nuts just because somebody says something about them."

"Have ya seen Slick lately?"

"He was going to press charges against you but I guess they told him to forget it. I better tell you this while I think of it. We're having a dinner party in Peace River and we want you guys to join us."

"What do you mean – a dinner party?"

"We're going to get a small banquet room in Peace River. The road's finished as far as the river so we're going to have a little celebration."

They went into the gas station. Chap was still on the phone.

Dayton leaned over the blueprint.

"Chap's thinkin' of expanding."

40

Coffee was boiling. Pancakes were burning. Leonard ran to the kitchen. Plopping two pancakes into a cereal bowl, he spread peanut butter and syrup on them and sat outside on the steps. Since moving into the house he had dusted and cleaned it to his satisfaction and had begun cleaning up the overgrown yard. A battered push mower, dragged up from the cellar, functioned as well as could have been expected as it chewed bite by laborious bite into knee-high quack grass. After several hours of cursing and kicking he had chiseled out a narrow trail where he could walk unhindered across the yard to the far end of a sagging clothesline. A paintless picket fence, leaning at a precarious angle, was destined for incineration.

It had taken a week, between jobs in the shop, to get the house painted. It was shinier than a dime. He had looked at a piece of property a couple of miles south of the gas station. The little house would fit perfectly inside a grove of cottonwood trees a long stone's throw from the highway. Maybe he could get Slick to go in with a Cat and carve out the building site. Maybe pigs fly.

A yellow leaf floated down beside him. It was getting cooler now, the days growing shorter. Chap had closed shop for the day so he and his wife could spend Thanksgiving with their daughter.

Thanksgiving. Lyla would have been helping her mother bake cookies. Thanksgiving and Christmas and first day of summer holidays were ordinary days now. There were no secret hiding places to find at Easter, no bicycle tires to patch or scabby knees to bandage. No special smells from the kitchen.

He had promised himself he would never again think of the note Maureen had left on the kitchen table. But it soaked his thoughts like rain on dry sod.

'Lyla was such a beautiful girl. I remember when you used to take her to the playground, pulling her in the wagon. "Faster, Dad!" I could hear you screeching and laughing from the end of the block. You would hurry then, your hair blowing in your face. When you got back home we would have a picnic in the backyard, under the tree you put the bird feeder in. Lyla liked it there. She liked being with you. You were the best father any father could be. When she went away you weren't the same. I could see how hard you tried to deal with it. You got your hair cut and went to church. You grew quieter. I saw how much you hurt and how much you had died inside. I saw how much you died when Lyla died. It was difficult for both of us when we lost her. But now it seems as if you're gone. I feel as if I've lost you both. You have always been the strong one in the family. Please be strong for me. Please be strong for Lyla and me.

I love you so much.'

XOXO

He finished eating the pancakes and went back to the kitchen for more. Returning to the back steps, he jammed one into his mouth with his fingers and washed it down with coffee. He'd buy the acreage he had looked at and put a white wishing well in the yard. For Lyla.

The breeze weakened. He sat against a tilting clothesline pole, closed his eyes and slipped into sleep.

***** ***** *****

"Leonard. Wake up!"

He craned his neck. It was Dayton.

"Mornin'. Must've dozed off there."

"How come it's closed?"

"It's Thanksgivin'."

"I need something to drink."

They went to the back door of the gas station. Leonard unlocked it and turned on the lights.

"Chap painted the ceiling," Dayton said.

"He got me a good deal on the house paint so I told him if I had any left over I'd paint the ceiling. I figured I'd set the house up someplace around here if I could find an acre or two. I was lookin' at a piece o' property south o' here. I think I'm gonna buy it. I'll have to get somebody to come in with a bulldozer to carve out a road and level off the house site, but it shouldn't take long to do that."

"It sounds like you're planning on staying here. What about your job in Kroywen?"

"As far as the house and acreage go, I'm lookin' at it as being more of an investment than anything. I'll get the yard cleaned up as much as I can before the snow flies and I'll stay in it for a while until I decide what I'm gonna do. I'm pickin' up a bit more work in the shop now and if it gets to the point where I'm gettin' half-decent paycheques I might start thinkin' seriously about stayin' here."

"Remember the dinner I was telling you about? Are you guys going to be there?"

"When hell freezes over."

"They know this has been kind of hard on you guys – how they had to go about getting the road to the river."

"All they had to do was talk to us. We could have moved the graves ourselves. None o' this bullshit would've happened."

"They had a job to do."

"They can't undo what they did. It's as simple as that. They can throw the biggest party known to man but it's not gonna undo what they did."

"What about Nestor? Can you talk to him about it?"

"I'm willin' to bet Nestor's more forgiving than most men, but I think you're pushin' it if you think he's gonna forgive you for all o' the crap that happened over the summer."

"They have to think about their public image. They could of lost shareholders if they would of found out they had bent the rules a little."

"Hang on a minute. This isn't so much about the company as it is about you, is it? It wouldn't surprise me if it was *your* idea to have this little shindig. You want to pull off this dinner thing to show 'em your powers of persuasion. You want to show 'em that you'll be a hell of a man to have in the Edmonton office."

"I can't do anything without you thinking that it has to be for the company. For my getting on with the company. Just because I want to get on board with these guys doesn't mean that everything I do is for them. I thought it would be a good idea for all of us to get together for a few hours and have a good time. But that's it."

"It's not that easy and you know it. A little dinner party doesn't change a damn thing. It'll be a frosty friggin' Friday when you see me sittin' in the same room as those clowns."

Dayton dug out his keys and headed for his truck. "I think you should talk to Nestor about it."

"Don't hold your breath."

41

Leonard's feet stuck out from under a truck. Chap pulled on one of his boots. "You better crawl out of there and take a break." He set a package of doughnuts and a travel mug of coffee on a small table in the corner of the shop. "You haven't been here all night, have you?"

"I was gonna do dishes and clean up the house a bit but it looked too much like work so I came here. I patched a couple o' tires and thought o' the fella who left his truck here for the transmission work. What time is it?"

"Eight thirty. Twenty seven past."

Leonard ripped open the doughnut package. "You're a good man."

"Are you having trouble with something?"

"There was some barbed wire wrapped around the driveshaft. I had quite a time gettin' it off. I saw that the pinion seal was leakin' a bit so I put in a new one. I sat outside for a while to take a little break and decided to get going on the tranny." He stuffed another doughnut into his mouth, washed it down with coffee and wiped off his moustache on the sleeve of his shirt. "How's the addition coming?"

"The demolition, you mean. We have to tear down part of a wall, where the addition's going to be. The outfit we're buying the house from gave us a bit of a deal on it. It shouldn't take long to get it inserted and nailed into place."

"Once a few truckers find out you've got a little soup and sandwich place happening you'll have big rigs stoppin' in."

"There's quite a bit of space out front we can use for parking. I'll have to get somebody to come in with a Bobcat or something to clean it up and level it off a bit."

"Once things get goin' you might have to hire extra staff."

"Blaine said she'd run it. She's been looking for an excuse to get out of Grande Prairie since her husband left. That's the main reason why I want to expand. If I can pick up a few extra bucks it'll be a bonus, but I'll be helping her out, too. She knows a lot about the business. It'll be a family project."

"Maybe you'll have a little more time for yourself. Get a little travelin' in."

"That's what she said. I have a brother in Digby. He's crippled up a bit from a car accident he was in a few years ago. Blaine says that once the snack bar is operational she's going to kick me and the wife out once a year whether we like it or not. She'll hire one of the young fellas from around here to watch the gas pumps while she does her thing with the sandwiches."

"Sure. If she's gonna run the sandwich end o' things you won't have to worry about having to do any extra work yourself to keep things goin'."

"That's right. It's too late in the season now to expect much interest in it, but a lot of big trucks go by every day. Like you said, once a few of them see that we have a coffee and sandwich joint here they'll stop to check it out. By spring we should be ready for the travelers."

Leonard stuffed another doughnut into his mouth. "I should be done here fairly soon."

"It can wait, Leonard. The only time I'd ask you to put in extra hours would be in an emergency." He stood at the front door. "It sounds like you bought yourself an acreage, according to what my realtor friend was saying."

"I did just that. I bought a two and a half acre parcel a couple o' miles south o' here. It's a nice little spot. I've got a Cat workin' on it now, knockin' down trees for the road. Once it's put in and the house site's cleared off I'll get a crew to come in and pour the foundation. I'll let it set for a bit before I haul the house over. I'll get a couple o' loads o' gravel for the road and that should about do it. Save a little yard work."

Nestor's truck pulled up. He climbed out.

"I better go. It looks like you've got company."

"Good morning, Chap."

"Good morning, good morning. There's some doughnuts on the table if you can get at them before Leonard finishes them off. I'll leave you guys alone."

"It looks like you're busy, Leonard. I shouldn't be taking up your time."

"No sweat. I need a little break."

Nestor swung a tattered chrome chair around and sat at the table. "The others went to Peace River to get a new stovepipe for the tent. I thought I'd run down to Edmonton for the heck of it and get a little practice driving in the big city. I was hoping you'd be interested in joining me. I didn't think you'd be working on a Sunday."

"I couldn't sleep so I came here. I'm not quite done yet. I'm going to have to pass on Edmonton. We'll go down when I'm a little more organized."

"How's the house coming? You must be about ready to move."

"I'm thinkin' it shouldn't take much more than a couple o' weeks to get settled in."

"I walked in a ways from the highway where the Cat's knocking down trees for the road. It's a nice little spot."

"Mark Twain said a few years ago they weren't makin' land anymore, so later on at some point it might be worth a few bucks."

"Is there anything I can get you when I'm in Edmonton?"

"I don't think so. When we go down together I might pick up a shirt or something but I don't need anything right now. How's Grin makin' out?"

"He's eating a little more now, and he's feeling better."

"Speaking of eating – Dayton told me the road crew bunch is having a dinner in Peace River some time soon. We're invited."

"Hoh boy. I don't know about that. We aren't very happy with what happened out there."

"Dayton asked me if I'd talk to you about it."

"They're going from one extreme to the other. They haven't shown any respect for us since day one and now they want us to join them for dinner. I don't even know if I should mention it to the old boys. They've had enough of their bullcrap. We all have, when you get right down to it."

"I can't argue with that. Next time I see Dayton I'll tell him they can eat by themselves."

"I don't imagine you see much of Dayton anymore, now that he's in Valleyview."

"I bumped into him in town one day when I made a run for parts. He isn't as excited about livin' in the trailer as he was before he moved in. He says they're usin' it to store parts. There's so much stuff in it, he said, that about the only room he has is a narrow channel between the bedroom and the kitchen.

There are grease pails and tires and everything under the sun piled halfway to the ceiling."

"The way you were talking before he was pretty excited that they had given him the trailer, but if they're using it to store parts he's probably trying to figure out what's going on."

"There's more. He's invested a good chunk o' change into a company contraption o' theirs. He's supposed to be goin' to go to some kind o' demonstration in Edmonton but they're having trouble gettin' everything put together properly so he hasn't had a chance to actually see what he spent all his money on. And I think you might be right. He might be beginning to get the idea they didn't give him the trailer after all. They just want to have him around to keep his eye on things and bring stuff out to camp when they need it. He said he was goin' half crazy because he couldn't watch TV for all the stuff that's piled up in the livin' room. And he's expected to sit around all day waitin' for the phone to ring."

Nestor dug the truck keys out of his pocket. "You did a great job putting the manifold in. It's quieter than a weasel now. I"ll have to wine and dine you when we get to the city."

"We'll go for burgers."

42

Leonard opened the bedroom dormer window. A gentle breeze swept tea towel curtains. He closed the envelope Nestor had left on the cup shelf in the shop and set it on the dresser. Pulling a book out of a cardboard box, he fluffed up his pillow and began reading.

Twenty seven pages later there was a knock on the back door. He stuck his head out the window. "C'mon in, Nestor. I'll be right down."

"I hope I'm not bothering you. I didn't think I'd be this late."

"No sweat." Leonard lit a lamp on the kitchen table, opened the back door and rolled a smoke. "What's up?"

"On the way to Edmonton I thought it would be a good idea to spend the night there, so I could have all day tomorrow to drive around, getting lost in traffic. But when I got there I didn't think I should waste my money on a motel if I didn't have to. I phoned Chap to tell him I was on my way back but would likely be late. I hope he didn't tell you it was an emergency."

"He said you were coming back later on and that you wanted to talk to me about something. But listen – before you get started – I'm a little confused about the envelope you left for me in the shop."

"All I can tell you is that Grin wanted you to have it. We all think you should know more about the graves. About Kawatina. The first day you were out at the lake, when you told us you had found the rocks, Allan and I talked about it when you were smoking in your sleeping bag. We were going to tell you more when we got out to the beaver pond, but Allan didn't feel right about Dayton. Before I say anything it might be easier if you tell me what you make of it because it must be a little confusing for you."

"I'll give it a whirl. After I found the rocks and matched them up with the boulders that are on the hill, I got to wondering why the boulders were only on one side o' the fire. I was curious as to why they wouldn't have put 'em *around* the fire instead of side by side, the way we see 'em now. I went back out there, got down on all fours and started crawling around. After I'd pulled away a bunch o' grass I grabbed the axe. It took quite a while but I ended up uncovering the tops of nine more boulders. The only thing that made sense to me was that the other boulders would have to represent nine more people. And if that was the case, there would have to be nine more graves out there somewhere. There's something that's been botherin' me, though. There are three exposed boulders on the hill. I can't figure out what the third one's doing there."

"All I can tell you is that the third boulder, the smallest one, represents Watina's father. Like you said, there are twelve boulders around the fire. There being a grave for each of the boulders is something we've often talked about."

"I'm not sure I understand what you're sayin'."

Nestor looked at the alarm clock on the stove. "I should be going. There's more I want to tell you but I wanted to be sure you'd be interested in hearing what I have to say."

"I'm interested as hell. Sometime soon we'll have to get together. By the way, Dayton stopped in at the shop after you left yesterday. He asked if I had talked to you about the dinner. He said the roadboys decided the right thing to do was respect the fact that Kawatina had nothing to do with them, so they aren't going to call the bridge the Kawatina bridge."

"I'm happy to hear that."

"Did you think about talkin' to the old boys about the dinner?"

"I told them we were invited to a little feed the road crew was having. When I turned in, they talked about it all night. In the morning they told me about the decision they had come to.

"What we have to do, they said, is hold on to what we have as a people and as a culture, and do everything we can to retain it. In this case they thought our presence would be important because by going to the dinner we would be showing them we haven't been defeated. We're aware of what they've done, but we have the constitution to stand up because we aren't going to go away as a result of their actions. By sitting in the same room, it will help send the message they'll be seeing more of us."

43

Dayton was drunk. He leaned toward Leonard, sitting beside him. "How often do you get the chance to sit with the executives of a big corporation? And drink their booze!?"

The lights had been dimmed in a small banquet room. Large candles rested on two tables, pushed together to form a T. The Suit was centred at the main table. Slick and KhakiPants filled the chairs on either side of him. KhakiPants chatted with The Suit. Slick sat quietly, his hands wrapped around a highball glass.

The campers occupied the second table. Leonard, uncomfortable out of his jeans and denim shirt, adjusted a cardigan sweater he had borrowed from Dayton. Across from him, Nestor sat between the old boys. Dayton stirred a martini with his finger. Leonard nursed a bottle of root beer. Nestor and the old boys drank Labrador tea Grin had brought in under his shirt. Old George, his long scraggly hair greased back, picked at embroidered flowers on the tablecloth.

"You better slow down, Dayton. That's your third martini. You already spent half the afternoon in the lounge with the roadboys."

"That's nothing!" he slurred. "I'm going to have three more. Just watch me." He finished the martini and faced Leonard. "The laser logger demonstration's going to be next week some time. You should come with me. You should get some shares while they're cheap. You'll make a killing on it. Like me."

"I think I'm better off spendin' my money getting the house set up on the acreage."

"All I know is that pretty soon pretty soon I'm going to be a rich man." He looked across the table. "What about you, Nestor? Are you going to be a rich man, too?"

"I'm already a rich man."

Dayton waddled around the main table and pulled his tie tight. "I just want to say how happy I am that we got the road completed across the river."

"Here here!" KhakiPants stood beside him, putting his arm on his shoulder. "Here's to a job well done."

Two waitresses came in, carrying large plates. Dayton returned to his chair.

"This looks good, boys." Knifing mixed vegetables onto a forkful of mashed potatoes, he aimed it toward his mouth, missing. A chunk of mashed potato clung to his chin. He leaned toward Leonard again. "There's not going to be any more canned stew for me. What about you, buddy?"

"I'm a stew man, myself. Give me a loaf o' brown bread and a couple o' cans o' stew and I'm happier than a magpie on roadkill."

KhakiPants pulled out a thick cigar and bit off the end. Leaning on the table to keep his balance, he lit the cigar on a candle. "We've got a little something for you fellas we think you'll be interested in." He gave everyone a small gift-wrapped box.

"Aren't ya gonna open them, for crying out loud?!" Slick stammered.

"I'm savin' mine for Christmas," Leonard said.

Dayton opened his. Inside was a silver cigarette lighter with the company logo etched into it. "I've always wanted one of these. This is perfect for you, Leonard."

"I'm savin' mine for Christmas." He pushed himself away from the table. "I seem to have lost my appetite." He headed for the coat rack in the corner of the room.

Grin stood up at the table. "I would like to thank you all for an extremely entertaining evening. But we'll have to be going now." He stuffed the gift into his shirt pocket and joined Leonard, waiting at the door.

44

Cardboard boxes filled with grease cartridges and oil filters cluttered a corner of the shop. Leonard took a bite out of a bologna sandwich and threw a piece of crust into a corner near a mouse hole. The sun-filled shop was cool and moist, heavy with the smell of grease, stale exhaust fumes, gasoline and cigarette smoke.

The phone rang.

"Hello."

"Hello, Leonard?"

"This is he."

"It's Dayton."

"Well, I'll be. I thought you'd died and gone to laser logger heaven."

"They screwed me on the laser logger."

"I'm not surprised. You shouldn't be, either. You know what they say about something that sounds too good to be true. I thought you'd start to get it figured out when they ended up usin' the trailer to store parts." He wedged the phone under his chin and rolled a smoke. "Things seemed to be goin' pretty good until those bozos started givin' you the idea you were gonna be workin' for 'em."

"I know you don't listen to the radio very much but I was wondering if you heard who the dead guy was."

"Who what dead guy was?"

"A body was found under a small bridge on a road construction site south of Valleyview. It was on the news this afternoon. I phoned a radio station in Peace River and a news guy told me that somebody lashed together a couple of logs to form an X and laid it across the road in front of the bridge. A gravel truck was highballing it down the road and almost wiped out. The truck driver found the body. The news guy said he couldn't say anything more about it."

"That was this afternoon, you say. When ya heard it on the radio."

"Around two o'clock."

"I'll go up there and see what I can find out."

Leonard high-tailed it up the highway. In a couple of hours he was back at the house. He fetched the envelope Nestor had previously left for him, went to the shop and sat at the coffee table. Half an hour later the phone rang.

"It's me," Dayton said. "I was wondering if you found out anything."

"I got back from Valleyview a while ago. They aren't releasing any information. So what's the story with your laser logger shares?"

"It was all bullshit. I think they made the laser logger shares up to give me the impression I was part of the company. They had to deal with the gravesite scenario so they probably thought it would be a good move if they had me to back them up about there not being any graves. By having me think I had my money invested in some new high technology equipment they knew I would do whatever they wanted me to do. I think they were afraid that they wouldn't get the road built to the river on time and they would end up losing some of their big investors. I've been thinking about it quite a bit and it makes sense to me."

"You were pretty happy the night of the little dinner party. All you could talk about was how rich you were going to be." Leonard dug a cigarette butt out of his pocket and waited for more.

"I ended up getting pretty sick. I didn't have any way of getting back to camp because I went to the roadcamp in my truck and then we all went to Peace River in the foreman's truck. I must of passed out because I woke up in a motel room. I was sick in bed all the next day. When I felt good enough to get up I had a shower and walked to the bus station. I had to wait until two o'clock in the morning to catch a bus to Valleyview."

"That's brutal. Treatin' ya the way they did. I had an idea something might be goin' on when you started talkin' about the laser logger all the time, but you were on cloud nine most o' the time and didn't want to listen to anything I had to say."

"It was pitch dark when I walked to the trailer court from the bus station. There was a chain with a lock on it across my driveway. My stuff was all over the lawn. They took everything I owned out of the trailer and threw it outside. They didn't pack it into boxes or anything. The phone was even gone. There was a note taped to the door. They wanted me to phone the head office as soon as I could. I changed into a clean shirt and pair of pants that were on the lawn. I had to phone the office from a payphone because the cell phone they gave me was gone. I was on hold for about ten minutes and I had to hang up because I didn't have enough change to pay for more long distance charges. When I phoned back after I got more change somebody I didn't know started talking to me. He said that he wasn't aware of an opening for an engineering job. Those guys told me all summer that they were going to do everything they could to get me the job, but there never was one. I did everything that they wanted me to do, including lying about the graves, but as soon as they got the bridge put in and we had the dinner party they didn't want to have anything to do with me."

"You'll have to get that straightened out. I gotta go. Call me in a few days."

Leonard looked again at three photographs that had been stuffed into the envelope Nestor had left for him. They were pictures of trees, no different than the thousands he had seen over the summer.

45

He sat up in bed and grabbed the alarm clock. Five thirty. He got dressed and went downstairs to the kitchen. The temperature had dropped considerably overnight. He lit Dayton's camp stove, filled the coffee pot with water, rolled a few cigarettes and shoved them into his shirt pocket. When the water was boiling he filled a travelmug with coffee and went outside. A slow, cool breeze greeted him.

Chap's extendable ladder was at the front of the gas station. He leaned it against the roof of the shop and got a chair from the coffee corner. Climbing onto the roof, sitting in the chair, he visualized Watina's fire burning

across the river in the dark distance. He
visualized the blue flame of the camp stove
burning the house down.

"Oh, shit!"

After warming up for a few minutes in
the house he walked over to the highway and
headed south. In an hour he was at the
acreage. The road into the house site was
sprinkled with large yellow leaves and smelled
of freshly-turned earth. He smoked a cigarette
under a tree, curled up and went to sleep.

Chap was sitting at the shop table when
he got back several hours later.

"Mornin'."

"Good morning, Leonard. It's been an
interesting morning around here."

"How's that?"

"Around nine o'clock a gal pulled in for
gas and asked me if I was a birdwatcher. An
hour or so later a couple of young bucks
stopped in for cigarettes and the one kid said I
could probably spot a lot of deer from up there.
When I was emptying the garbage outside, I
saw it." Chap went out the door and motioned
for Leonard to follow. He pointed up at the
peak of the roof. "You wouldn't have any idea
how that chair could have made its way up
there, would you? You must be hungry. The

wife knows you like apple pie. She baked one last night. We better check it out."

They went into the gas station, Leonard glancing back once.

Neither of them spoke until they had finished eating. They went outside and sat on a pile of two by fours.

"You were out walking, were you?"

"Hiked down to the acreage."

"The RCMP were here earlier. Did you hear what happened?"

"Dayton phoned yesterday. He heard something on the radio about a body bein' found. I went to Valleyview to talk to the RCMP about it. The body was under a small bridge crossing one o' the creeks near the muskeg. Did they give you any idea who it might be?"

"They were only here for a few minutes."

"I'd like to talk to Nestor about it."

"He was here, looking for you. I told him I wasn't sure where you were but that you'd probably be at the acreage."

"Did he say where he was goin'?"

"No, but he's going to phone you later."

Several hours later Leonard was having a nap in the shop when Nestor called.

"I know you probably have other things to do," he said, "but I was wondering if you wouldn't mind meeting me. Later on. I have a few things to take care of right now but I can be in Valleyview in a couple of hours."

"I'll meet you at the truck stop."

*****   *****   *****

Nestor was slumped at a booth. He rested his head in his hand. "You must have heard what happened."

"Dayton phoned. He told me."

"The body hasn't been identified yet."

"Any idea who it is?"

Nestor spoke quietly, although the restaurant was empty. "I phoned the detachment this afternoon and the constable said they'd like to talk to a relative or close friend. I'm not too big on going into police stations and was wondering if you wouldn't mind going in."

"What about George?"

"I don't know where he is."

"Sure, I'll go in."

"They gave me a phone number." Nestor dug into his shirt pocket. "You might not see me for a while. There are some things I have to do."

46

Tobacco, cigarette papers, spilled coffee and toast crumbs littered the kitchen table. A new naphtha gas lantern hummed above him. His gut had been right. It was Grin he had seen earlier on. On a cold table.

The RCMP had shown him nine photographs they found taped to his chest. They were similar to the three photos from Nestor's envelope he was looking at now.

Going to the window, he looked outside, immersed in thought.

47

He leaned against the thin tamarack rail at the cemetery. A cold wind scraped his cleanly-shaven face. The black suit again hung uncomfortably. Nestor and the minister were gone. The bell in the small chapel had stopped chiming. Nestor had built a cross, painted it and planted it above Grin's head. Allan's grave was beside his.

He turned and walked back to the truck, half a mile ahead of him.

48

He crawled out of bed and looked through an early window. Cottonwood trees shivered in a cool breeze. He got dressed, put the coffee on and went outside. It would take all day to clean up scattered branches and roots cluttering his new yard. The photographs Nestor had left for him were on the kitchen table. Filling his mug with coffee, he went back outside. He'd build a wishing well after the yard had been cleaned up. Digging a hoe out from under a tarpaulin, he began working the fresh soil.

By late afternoon two piles of roots and branches had been burned. He had asked them to leave as many trees standing as possible. The house had been coaxed onto the foundation. Branches poked the walls and roof.

He had more work to do. At the hill. He gathered a few things from the house and drove to the gas station.

Chap was out back. Dots of sweat covered his head. "Hello there, Leonard. I thought I'd clean up a bit back here."

"You don't have to do that. I can get it in a few days. I'll tear down the fence and burn it. It probably wouldn't hurt to yank the clothesline poles out."

"Don't worry about that. It's none of your concern."

"I was thinkin' maybe I could salvage a few o' the fence pickets and use 'em to make a bookshelf for the house. If I sand 'em down and put a little varnish on 'em I think they'll add a little character to the living room. Is anything going to be happenin' in the shop over the next few days? I was thinking of taking off with the canoe for a while and doing a little walleye fishin'."

"No, unfortunately there's nothing I can keep you busy with. But something's come up. The other mechanic took a turn for the worse a few days ago. He complained about having a stomach ache so I sent him home early. It sounds like he's experiencing some complications of some sort from the surgery he had a while ago. The doctor doesn't want him to twist wrenches anymore. He doesn't think it's serious so he's going to keep working in the shop. But I wanted to let you know that he might have to hang up his coveralls permanently one of these days, and I'd like you to take his place full time if there's any way I can get you to stay."

"I'll have to give that some serious thought."

"You've been working on the house every day that you haven't been in the shop, so it'll probably do you some good to get out of here for a while."

"Have you seen my axe around here anywhere? I thought I had it at the acreage but I couldn't find it."

"It's probably in the corner of the storage room. I think they were using it outside."

Leonard turned to leave. "I'm going to head out first thing in the morning. I'll probably be two or three days, depending on how the fishin' goes."

49

He hunched over a small fire and watched a crow waddle along the edge of the borrow pit. He recalled having sat under a tree in the pouring rain, trying to roll a cigarette, with a dead finger pointing at him.

He dug out the photos he had stuffed under his shirt. They were photographs of trees. Of the thousands of trees surrounding him, he had to find the ones that were in the photographs. Pulling on his packsack, he started walking.

An hour had passed when he stopped for a break. He again fanned out the photographs, wondering for the hundredth time why Nestor had left the envelope on the coffee cup shelf in the shop instead of giving it to him directly.

He continued walking. It was late afternoon when red and yellow survey ribbons tied to scattered trees indicated he was inside the timber berth. This was where the road was headed. Where the trees would fall.

By early evening he reached the crest of a small sand esker. Rocks had been piled beside an old fire. He pulled them down, uncovering a piece of thin, folded cardboard. One, two, three, four, five… seventeen Xs had been sketched onto a crude map.

Holy smokes. I'm gonna die here.

50

He trudged to the shop, unlocked it and went in. His sleeping bag was under the coffee table. He rolled it out in the mouse hole corner and crashed.

Chap's feet crunched against frosty gravel at six thirty. He knocked twice and stuck his head in the door. "Leonard. Is that you?"

"C'mon in."

"You scared the daylights out of me. I didn't see any lights on in here a few minutes ago. And your truck isn't here. I thought someone was trying to break in."

Leonard's voice was thick and gravelly. "I got in early this mornin'."

"Where's your truck?"

"I had a little breakdown. Nothin' serious, but it was too dark to take a look at it and I didn't have any tools with me. So I walked back. I think it's a plugged fuel filter. It won't take but half an hour to replace it. If you'd be interested in cookin' up some sausages and eggs I know someone who'd be interested in eatin' 'em."

"Sure thing. How far did you have to walk?"

"Just up the road a ways. A mile or so."

Chap turned to leave. "I'll have your breakfast ready in twenty minutes."

Leonard stripped off and unwrapped a rag from his thigh. He cleaned out a long gash with stinging, soapy water.

Breakfast was on the counter when he limped in. Chap filled two coffee cups. "You look a little wobbly this morning."

"An old knee injury that bothers me now and then."

"Besides having gas problems last night, how was the fishing?"

"I got sidetracked a bit. I bumped into an old fella changin' a flat tire at a boat launch and gave him a hand. We got to talkin' about one thing and another and he said the motor was just about gone in his truck. He'd have to sell an aluminum boat and nine horsepower motor he has sittin' in his back yard to come up with the money to pay for a new one. I told him I was a mechanic and could put a good used motor in for him in trade for the boat and motor. He said I was the answer to his prayers. Would there be any problem with my usin' the shop for a couple o' days or so to get the old boy goin?"

"No, I don't think so. Something might come up and I might need you for a job, but I don't imagine the old fella will be too worried if it takes an extra day or two. I'll run you down to your truck after you finish eating. Give me a holler when you're ready. I'll be in the back room."

51

Nestor dug a quarter out of his pocket and dropped it into a freshly-painted wishing well.

"Don't tell anybody what your wish is, or it won't come true."

Nestor walked toward the back of the house.

"I'm up on the roof. The ladder's at the back door."

Nestor joined him. Purple-pink clouds smudged the sun. "This is really something, isn't it?"

Leonard pointed. "And look at that."

Nestor held his hand against the late sun. "You can see the hill. It sticks out like a sore thumb from here."

"I'll bet if you had a set of binoculars you could see the house from there. I thought I might have paid a little too much for the acreage, but with a rooftop view like this I've changed my mind. I'm thinkin' I might build some kind of deck up here if I can figure out how to do it. I was about to make some coffee when you pulled in." They climbed down and went inside. Leonard lit a lantern. "I'm going to have to get the chimney cleaned pretty soon. It's startin' to get a little chilly in the evenings now. The lantern's about the only heat I have in here. Chap was saying there's some kind of Arctic high headed this way. And one o' these days winter's gonna put its legs down."

"I wouldn't be surprised to see snow one of these days."

"There's something I've been thinkin' about."

Nestor waited.

"There were two Kawatina symbols drawn in the upper corner of the envelope you left for me. I don't know if it's worth mentioning but I've been wondering why they're there."

"I was happy to see that Grin had drawn them in. It's something we've talked about for a long time. We don't think First Nations people should have to use postage stamps. We were here long before there was a postal system in this country. We think it's an intrusion on our inherent rights that we should be expected to use a structure that's alien to us. It's another white thing that has been shoved down our throats."

"But what about this – if natives wouldn't be required to use postage stamps, a *lot* o' people wouldn't use them because there would be no way of knowin' who sent the letter."

"To get around the possibility of having white people suddenly turn red in order to avoid having to buy a stamp, we thought the best solution would be to have every Indian band in the country have its own Federally-registered postage logo. Every Post Office in each respective band would have one. It would essentially be a rubber stamp. Every native Indian in the country could write letters without having to worry about putting a stamp on the envelope."

"So on Grin's envelope – the one you left me – the Kawatina symbol in the corner represents a native stamp."

"Yes. And I think he took it a step further. He put two Kawatina symbols in the corner, one overlapping the other. I think that was his way of indicating that the contents of the envelope were important, like it was a First Class letter."

"Did Allan talk to anybody about the possibility of actually doing it? Getting it set up?"

"He knew better than that. It's one thing to have a good idea, but reality tends to shadow a lot of good ideas. We're still waiting for the Federal government to honour treaties that were signed in the eighteen hundreds. Allan didn't think there was much point in approaching them about developing a specific native postage stamp when they have cardboard boxes full of treaty material from two centuries ago that haven't been addressed properly. It won't be long before I'll be out of this neck of the woods for the winter. I think it would be good if we could spend a little more time on the hill. It'll give you a chance to get caught up on anything you might have questions about."

"Sounds good. I still have to go to the campsite one o' these days and clean it up a bit."

"We should go as soon as we can if it's going to get colder."

"The shop's closed on weekends, so that would be best. We'll spend the night there."

"I have a few things to get caught up on. How about we make it two weekends from now?"

"Sure. That works for me."

52

The mouse skittered across the floor and disappeared behind a stack of boxes. Leonard, down on all fours, inched toward a peanut and waited. The mouse returned, chomped into it and raced to a corner.

"You're welcome, Mick."

Returning to his broom, he piled sweepings beside a garbage pail and covered them with a cardboard box. Chap's whistling penetrated the open door.

"Leonard, my good man, I was wondering if you could do me a favour."

"What's up?"

"I've been putting off cleaning up the addition but today I thought I better get with it. A bunch of wood scraps and insulation pieces slipped off the back of the truck when I was leaving to go to the dump this morning. The wind scattered them all over the far end of the area we're going to use as a parking lot. I'd appreciate it if you could get everything picked up and put in the trash barrel."

"I'll get a man on that right away."

They stepped outside. "The carpenters like your chair on the roof. They want to nail it down permanently. We have a reception to go to tonight. I'm going to close up now. Is there anything I can get you?"

Leonard pulled a twenty out of his pocket. "Pick me up a pouch o' that Dutch tobacco, wouldja?"

Chap slipped into his car and drove off. A gust of wind scattered several pieces of insulation. Another blast whipped dust into Leonard's eyes. He went to the far end of the parking area and, fetching a long stick, poked at a garbage bag hung up on a tree branch.

A cloud of cold dust filled the lot. Dayton's truck stopped in front of the shop. Dayton got out.

"I'll just be a minute." Gathering small pieces of trash, Leonard bunched them up and stuffed them into the garbage barrel.

Dayton got back into his truck and unrolled the window. "How come the gas station's closed?"

"Chap's goin' to some kind of anniversary or something." Leonard scooped up the last of the wood pieces, brushed his hands on his jeans and squatted behind the truck to roll a smoke. "Have you got a lighter in there?"

Dayton jabbed the cigarette lighter and chugged on a can of pop.

"Before I forget," Leonard said, "I got a new lantern so I don't need yours anymore. It didn't work very well. The wick was stuck down inside and I couldn't pull it out. Hang on a minute and I'll get it from the shop. I'm gonna keep the camp stove for a while if you don't mind. It's the only thing I've got to heat up the kitchen 'til I get the chimney cleaned." He hobbled to the shop and returned with the lamp.

"It wouldn't be that hard for Chap to put a coin-operated pop machine outside, so a guy could get a drink when he wanted to."

"I haven't seen ya for a while. Have you had a chance to talk to those goofballs about your shares?"

"Whenever I phone the Timbco office I get the runaround and nobody knows what I'm talking about. When I was in the trailer they told me I could have the computer they were using for the job once the road was completed to the river. They said they'd leave it at the front desk of the motel. I phoned there yesterday and the lady on the phone said that it was there and I told her I'd be coming up to get it. I just got back from there and the guy who was at the front desk told me that last night the foreman showed up drunk and he took it with him."

"So ya drove all the way up here for nothin'."

"When I phoned you before I didn't tell you what they said after they kicked me out of the trailer. I phoned the main office to find out what was going on. I ended up talking to somebody who said that the best thing to do would be to come in to the main office and they would be able to answer any questions I had. So I drove all the way to Edmonton. There were two guys that said they worked for a contract public relations company. They weren't even company guys. They said that sometimes in business you have to do things you don't normally do in order to reach your quarterly goals. They said that they would talk to the appropriate staff about it and that I could expect to get a cheque in the mail. But I still haven't got it."

"It was obvious to me KhaiPants was intent on getting you interested in joinin' ranks with 'em. When he started talkin' to ya about the engineering job in the main office it didn't take long before you and him were closer than balls. It was Grin who got the inside information on the laser logger. He told Nestor it was somethin' they had cooked up so they could get you on board to make it easier for them to dig up the gravesite. So they could use you to cover their butts. You did a pretty good job. I'll give you credit for that. You were about as friendly as a dog on a bone, defending 'em. Your eyes lit up like casino lights every time you talked about the laser logger."

"How did Grin find out about it?"

"The roadboys got him to take 'em out fishing one day, Nestor said. I think they paid him fifty bucks. They were out in the boat all day fishin' and hootin' and howlin' and having a wonderful time. For shore lunch Grin cooked 'em up a walleye and French fries. While he was cookin' they sat at the fire and had a few beers. They thought it was hilarious how anybody could be so gullible as to think there could be such a thing as a laser logger. Meanwhile, Grin's bumbling around, spillin' grease on his shoe, tippin' over the coffee pot and stuff like that, learning all about the bogus laser logger and findin' out firsthand what a bunch o' ying yangs they are."

"You knew this was going on and you didn't even have the decency to tell me!"

"I didn't know for sure it was all bullshit until later on. And who the hell are you to be talkin' about decency? You saw what they did out there and you didn't do a friggin' thing to try to stop 'em because all you gave a damn about was yourself. All ya gave a damn about was getting rich. Once they started butterin' you up about a job in the office you were hangin' onto 'em like a burr on a Spaniel's ass. That's why they conjured up all the laser logger bullshit. They knew if they could get their meathooks into ya, you'd do whatever they wanted."

"I suppose you think it's a big joke."

"What went on out there wasn't a joke. Besides seein' the gravesite get destroyed I lost three friends."

"What do you mean, three?"

"Allan and Grin and George.   One two three."

"George is still here."

"He vanished when Grin died.   He showed up for the funeral and now he's gone."

"I can tell you this much. I might of got screwed with the shares and the engineering job, but they know I did a hell of a job covering their butts for them."

"I'll tell ya something else.   Slick dumped the pods into the river. I know what I'm talkin' about because I saw it with my own eyes. I spent the day fishin' in the river and stayed overnight on the hill. I was sittin' at the fire when Slick showed up on a bulldozer. He dug up both pods and dumped 'em in the river. They're under ten or twelve feet o' water. Maybe some day they'll spread a couple o' loads o' gravel over 'em to cover 'em up. But that's where they are, anyway. I'll bet nobody told you about that."

"They can say the pods were already in the river and they have no idea what they are or where they came from."

"But I have a chunk o' cement up in my room. *Pod* cement. And I'll tell ya something else.   Grin was one o' the most intelligent people I've ever met. Do you remember what he told you the night o' the dinner? When you were knockin' back dry martinis? You probably don't 'cuz you were pissed to the gills. He said 'I might be an old Indian but I'm not a dumb Indian.' He wasn't a dumb Indian by any stretch o' the imagination. He was up in the hills when all this bullshit was comin' down. And he was watchin'."

"So what? He's dead. Dead people can't talk."

"Here's something else for you. Do you remember I mentioned to you one day that I was readin' about dirty money? That's your money, man. *Dirty* money. If ya get money by lying and takin' advantage o' people, it's dirty money. It doesn't get any dirtier than that as far as I'm concerned. I can understand you're bein' upset about the possibility of losing your 'hard-earned money', as you call it, but maybe this is the way it was meant to be. Maybe you were supposed to go through all this bullcrap so it would bring you to your senses a bit."

"Speaking of money, it's a long drive to get back home and you still owe me gas money for when you and Nestor took the truck to Fox Creek to get some stuff for the old guys. You probably don't even remember that."

"I do, as a matter o' fact." He dug into his pocket. "I must have forgotten about all the money I've been givin' ya for groceries. For both of us. Not just me. And all the gas I put in the truck. And I must have forgotten about the brake shoes I bought for your new truck here and ya haven't even had 'em put in yet."

"You said you were going to do that."

Leonard opened the tailgate of the truck and dumped crumpled bills and loose change from his pocket. The wind picked up a five dollar bill. Leonard chased it down and set a rock on the bills. "That's all I have. There ya be."

Dayton scooped up the money and jammed it into his jacket pocket. He slammed the tailgate shut, jumped into the truck and sped out, filling the air with dust and gravel.

Turning his back to the wind, Leonard limped to the shop.

53

Leonard leaned against a boulder. Orange coals glowed in the fire pit.

They had royally screwed Dayton with the laser logger. They had sucked him in like a hair down a drainpipe. "But you sucked *them* in, Grin. 'I might be an old Indian, but I'm not a dumb Indian'."

"I hope you're cooking French fries, because I'm starving."

Leonard turned. It was Nestor.

"I didn't hear ya comin, my friend."

"I wanted to walk up here on the game trails. Like we did all summer. It took longer than I thought it would. My legs are a little stiff."

"I caught a nice pike in the river. It should be ready to eat pretty soon."

Nestor leaned his packsack on the woodpile. "I see you have Grin's bow saw. He knew you'd bring it back if you found the tree he had cut down with it."

"I don't know how in the world the old boy could cut down a tree three feet thick with a bow saw, but he did. He drew up a little map on Timbco's timber berth showin' the location of seventeen trees, and stuck it under a rock pile beside the fire he'd been sittin' at. When I was hikin' around the country I stopped for a smoke at the esker, pulled down the rock pile and found it. I didn't have a lot o' time on my hands but I managed to track three of 'em down. They have to be three o' the biggest trees in the country. He had 'em marked with pieces of red survey ribbon. I'm looking forward to finding the rest of 'em when I have the time."

An hour later they had finished eating. "What's up for you now, Leonard? Do you have any plans?"

"Chap mentioned that the other mechanic might not be stickin' around much longer. He's got gut problems the doctors are worried about. Chap asked me if I'd be willing to work full time if he can't come back, and I told him I'd think about it. I have a pretty good job in Kroywen, and they seem to be happy enough with the work I've been doin', so I'm going to have to give it some serious thought. But I'm beginnin' to like the idea of stayin' here, to be honest with you. The way Chap was talkin' it sounds like I've got a full-time job if I want it, and now that the acreage is cleaned up a bit I can see getting settled in. And like I was just sayin' – there's fourteen more trees on Grin's map that have to be found. I think out of respect I should find 'em. I owe the old boy that much."

"If you hadn't been here to help us out with the gravesite scenario I don't know what we would have done."

"I have something I want to show you."

Nestor followed Leonard to the edge of the hill. Leonard moved two logs and pulled up a plastic bag. "This is for you."

Nestor opened the bag. His eyes widened. "The headstones!"

"When I first found the graves and uncovered them I brought them up here because I wanted to compare them with the boulders. When I could see they were essentially the same I went back across the river and put 'em back where they belonged. I was gonna leave 'em there, but when the roadboys indicated they might end up having to dig up the graves I came back and got them. I want you to have them because this is your business, not mine."

"When you told Allan and me you had put them back I thought that was the end of them." He peered into the bag again. "This is really something. I know Allan will feel better, knowing they're safe."

Leonard went back to the fire and pulled an old work shirt out of the woodpile. Unwrapping it, he pulled out a large blue handkerchief, the corners tied together. He gave it to Nestor.

"I think I know what it is. This is the same kind of handkerchief you gave Grin at the lake when you were fishing in your canoe." He opened it. "It's Watina. It's Watina's hand."

"When I was at the lake I gave Grin one of the hands to give you an idea I had the other one. So you'd know she was being taken care of. But there's more. I have to fess up and admit I didn't tell you everything that happened the night I went in to talk to the cops. It might be a little confusing because sometimes I don't do a very good job of explainin' things. I'll take a run at it and you can interrupt me if you have trouble followin' me.

"You might already know this, but there were nine photographs taped to Grin's chest. Nine photographs of trees, like the ones that were in the envelope you left for me at the shop. When I went in to talk to the cops they asked me if I knew anything about them and I told 'em in all honesty I didn't. I ended up sittin' in their waiting room for the longest time, looking at pictures o' trees.

"It wasn't until I got back home after talkin' to the RCMP that things started falling into place a little. I had an idea there was something Grin wanted me to be aware of and that was why he left three of the photos with you to give to me. The photos that were in the envelope had the Kawatina symbol drawn on the back of each one, but the ones at the police station didn't have anything on 'em. I knew that before I could take it any further I would have to have all the photos, not just the three that were in the envelope. I went back to the detachment and asked if I could get duplicates of the photos that were taped to Grin's chest. They were good enough to give me copies of all o' them.

"It took a while, but after a lot o' shuffling I could see that the pictures overlapped each other. He took the pictures in such a fashion that if you stood in the location of where he took the first one and you overlapped the second one onto the first one and made your way to that spot, all you had to do was overlap the next picture and start walkin' again and then overlap the next one until you got to the end. It was Grin's way of creating a little roadmap of sorts.

"I told Chap I was goin' fishing for a few days and headed for the borrow pit. I had an idea it was where Grin started takin' pictures. And I was right. It was where I had reburied the bodies – where you and Allan and I went and discovered they had been dug up again. There's a thick stand of poplar in there so it took a while to get everything lined up properly before I could get started. It took me the better part o' the day to make my way to the last one."

"I'm glad you were able to figure it out. Grin knew he was going to die this summer. When we lost Allan he knew I was the only one left, besides you and George, who knew about Kawatina. He might have wanted to give you the opportunity to get a better feel for it, if you were interested."

"So rather than come right out and tell me certain things, he left some clues for me to follow."

Nestor nodded. "And I think that's why he marked those big trees. To give you an idea of how important they were to our people."

"Did you know about the photos? Did you know he was takin' 'em?"

"He had me buy a roll of film from the gas station. I thought it was unusual because he never took a picture in his life. The only reason he had a camera in the first place was because it was given to him years ago, and when the house burned down it was one of the few things he managed to salvage. But I knew he was up to something when I saw that the camera was missing from the tent. When he gave me the envelope to give to you I had an idea there were photos in it."

"I was pretty choked up after I saw him on the table at the morgue. Seeing Allan in a pine box was bad enough but when I saw Grin lying there, grinnin' at me, I had a little trouble keepin' it together. I ended up goin' to the RCMP with Watina's hand in a coffee can."

"You what?"

"I better rephrase that. I was going to lay the whole thing on the RCMP and tell 'em how they dug up the graves and the whole nine yards. But I ended up sittin' on the curb on the other side o' the street. I drank a thermos o' coffee, tryin' to figure things out. My pants were soakin' wet and I was colder than a Creamsicle so I took it as a sign it would be best to keep my mouth shut."

"I'm happy to hear you didn't tell them anything. It might have made things more complicated than they already are. It's going to be dark soon. It gets a liitle cool up here some nights."

"I brought blankets with me. I'll be all right."

Nestor looked eastward, along the new road. "Where's your truck?"

"Parked in the trees. Not far from here."

"I'd like to tell you more about Kawatina, but we could be up all night."

"No sweat. Get started and I'll build up the fire."

"Several years ago Allan wanted me to come with him out here to the river. That was when he showed me the graves."

"Do you have any idea who else would've known about 'em? I would have to think someone must have shown them to him."

"He never did say how he found out about them. The best way to describe them would be to say that they're lost graves. Graves that have been lost track of."

"But I'm still a little confused. How do Watina and Kawutinee fit into this? Their names, I mean. If they're lost graves how would you know their names?"

"That's one of the things I want to explain to you. Watina and Kawutinee are names Allan created for the people in the graves."

"If that's the case I can't help but wonder if it's actually a mother and daughter buried there."

"He never did explain why the graves represented a mother and daughter."

"The story about Watina and Kawutinee picking berries along the river sounds authentic enough."

"Allan said it wasn't enough for him to know about the graves without knowing about the people who were in them. That's why he created the story about Watina and Kawutinee. We have to give him credit – he came up with an interesting story. But what's important is that it doesn't matter that Kawatina is Allan's creation. What is important is that because of him the graves haven't been forgotten. The people resting there haven't been forgotten."

"I would have to assume, then, he accidentally discovered the graves."

"Like the old boys say – it's Allan's story and everything belongs to him."

"And he created the names for the people buried there."

"Yes. And he combined parts of each of their names to create 'Kawatina'. On top of that he was the one who came up with the symbol – the Kawatina symbol – to represent the hill and sacred ground."

"I'm comfortable enough with that. But what about the boulders on the hill? I know two of 'em are tied to the graves because the rings on the boulders are the same as the rings on the headstones I found near the river. And the way you explained it, the third exposed boulder is Watina's father. The only thing that made sense to me about the other boulders was that they must represent nine more graves. I was dead-set on findin' 'em so I grabbed my axe and went down to river level and started diggin'. But all I found was wild strawberries."

"I'm going to sidetrack a bit here. Allan created another story to illustrate the importance of the boulders on the hill. There are twelve boulders here. They all represent seasons. So twelve boulders would represent twelve seasons. The two large exposed boulders represent spring and summer. They're both fully exposed to indicate that those seasons have passed. The third boulder

– the one that isn't fully exposed – represents autumn. It isn't fully exposed because it represents the season Earth is in now. We are in the season of harvest, and the season of harvest isn't over. The forests and seas, the mines and oil reefs are all being harvested. It is a good season in the minds of those interested in reaping as much as they can from the earth. There are still many forests to cut down and many fish to drag out of the sea before the harvest season is over. The way Allan tells it once everything has been harvested the third boulder will be totally exposed because the season of harvest will be over. There will be nothing left to harvest because Earth will have been stripped of its natural resources.

"The point Allan wanted to put across was that now is the time we have to be careful not to allow greed to terminate Earth's harvest season prematurely. If we stop our incessant harvesting now, if we put a stop to our greed before it's too late, we can redirect our actions toward issues we have thoughtlessly neglected in the past, and in doing so will allow Earth to revive."

"Holy Smokes. It might take a week or two to digest that one."

"Allan often thought 'out of the box', as they say. In many ways he was ahead of the pack with the things he chose to think about. If you end up staying here I'll tell you about his view of things if we continue to allow greed to control the way we live. He called it 'Kouetta'.

"Another thing important to him was that in order to properly respect the people who are at rest here the area around the hill should be recognized as sacred ground. The roadguy who always wears a fancy suit didn't realize how accurate he was when he made the comment that there was no way there could be a boundary for the sacred ground when about the only things our people owned back then to mark a boundary with were bows and arrows. The way Allan liked to tell it, that was exactly what they *did* use to create the sacred boundary. Over the generations arrows were shot out into the bush from each of the twelve boulders around the fire whenever there was a burial. A general boundary was created where hundreds of arrows had been shot into the bush over the years. Over a period of time the hill became the central point of the sacred ground.

"The dreams Watina had of fires burning was a glimpse of what was happening to the earth – through industrialization and greed it was slowly being consumed by fire. Allan's thinking was that by creating a boundary for the sacred ground everyone within the boundary would be spared from the fire. That was why it was so important to him. It was his way of knowing our people would be protected. The fact that our relatives who were here before us wrestled large sandstone boulders to the top of the hill verifies that the area was extremely important to them. It's all in Kouetta. You'll have to wait until I get a break from university before I can tell you the complete story." Nestor rolled out his blankets and fastened the top button of his shirt. "That's all I can give you for now. It's probably going to be a bit chilly tonight." He stretched out and pulled a blanket over his head.

Leonard twisted up a smoke and gazed at the river below them. He had a lot to think about.

54

At daybreak they huddled behind a moody fire. It had cooled considerably overnight. Large, vagrant snowflakes sputtered against dull flames. They had a quick breakfast of coffee and Nestor's fig newtons and filled their thermoses.

"Let's go for a walk," Leonard said.

"I noticed last night that your leg's still bothering you."

"I slipped the other day walkin' along the edge of a creek and fell into a dead branch sticking out o' the water. I put a poultice on it with a recipe I dreamt up but I think I might have waited a little too long and it got ahead o' me."

"Let's take a look at it."

Leonard pulled down his jeans, unwrapped a rag strip and exposed a sizeable chunk of purple flesh, oozing and partly crusted over.

"That doesn't look too good, Leonard. It might be infected."

"When I get back I'll have a long shower and doctor it up a bit."

They made their way down the hill and headed for the bridge. Leonard led the way and peered into the water below him. "It's cloudy and dark today. I don't know if we're going to see anything down there."

Nestor squinted and looked from side to side, unsure of what he was looking for.

Several minutes passed. "Over here, Nestor. Take a look down here."

"What am I looking for?"

"The pods. They're right below us."

Nestor stood beside him and squinted harder, his eyes thick slits in his forehead. "I don't know what they look like."

"Keep lookin' and you'll see something that looks like a cement coffin."

"It looks like something starts to take shape but the current carries the image away."

"It's not a very good day to see 'em, but they're down there. I think they thought they'd be invisible under the water. But they didn't think I'd be watching them put 'em there."

Nestor squinted down into the water again, his eyes two thin lines across his forehead.

"I've got more," Leonard said. "We may as well leave the packs under the bridge."

They walked a couple of hundred yards, stopping where the spur road leading to the borrow pit intersected the logging road. Leonard pulled a single photograph from his shirt pocket and held it up. "Take a look at this."

Nestor held up the photo and compared the baring trees in front of him to what he was looking at in the photo.

"This is where the trail ends," Leonard said. "They had Muskeg Marty out here watchin' us, takin' pictures of me when I busted open the pods. But what they didn't know was that Grin was out here watching *them*, takin' a few pictures of his own."

"So the bodies are…"

"A hundred yards back in the bush. I dug 'em up from here, where KhakiPants had buried 'em, and reburied 'em again. Here's something else I found." Nestor followed him to a tree. Several toothpicks had been wedged into the rough bark. "KhakiPants is the only person around here I know of who chews on toothpicks. That gives us a pretty good idea of who did the shovel work."

Nestor followed Leonard into the trees. "I reburied them here." The ground appeared undisturbed. "It took all day, but nobody's gonna find 'em now."

"Now I know where to put Watina and the headstones."

A cold breeze crept up on them. "I think that Arctic front's arrived. Let's get back to the bridge."

Leonard favoured his leg. They walked slowly. Reaching the bridge, they went below and dug the thermoses out of their packs.

"Well Nestor, I guess we're gonna be going our separate ways."

"Yes. It's time to get on with other things. I feel a little guilty, though. You came here to do some fishing and got tangled up with us."

"I learned a lot about a lot o' things this summer. And I met some damn fine people in the process."

Nestor opened his packsack and pulled out a folded blue bandana. "This is for you."

Leonard untied the corners. An intricately-carved raven the size of his fist stared at him with beady eyes.

Leonard ran his fingers over perfect feathers. "Allan must have made this."

"I made it. When I saw how gruesome your raven slingshot looked I thought a raven carving would remind you of some of the lighter moments you had over the summer, as few as they were."

Leonard held up the carving. The eyes, small yellow stones, glistened in the dull day. "I saw a lot of Allan's stuff over the summer and could see he had a real talent for it, but this is a lot better than his stuff."

"I started carving in my teens. One day Allan was whittling a stick and I showed him a few things. It didn't take him long to get interested in it. It was a good outlet for him. I gave him a couple of good knives and showed him how to work the grain of the wood. It didn't take long before he was carving some nice stuff. After he died I thought I should carve one more piece, and a raven seemed appropriate." He pulled a knife out of his pocket. "This is for you, too. I won't be doing any carving now and I'd like you to have it."

"Thank you. I appreciate that." Leonard dug a set of keys out of his jeans. "Take the truck back. I'm gonna spend one more night on the hill. I have a lot to think about."

"I walked here and I'm going to walk back. You have a bad leg."

"I'll look after it when I get back to the house. I need one more night on the hill." He cut a walking stick from a nearby grove of willows. They went to his truck, parked in the bush a short distance from the bridge. "I'm not much for goodbyes, Nestor. Leave an address and phone number with Chap when you get settled."

Nestor started the truck. "I'll phone you at the garage next week." He headed toward the highway.

Leonard went back to the bridge and cut a sleeve off his shirt. Tearing it into strips he soaked them in cold river water and wrapped them around his bad leg.

It was an hour before he reached the crest of the hill. *Every step I take…* He drank hard from a water bag and sat on the smallest boulder – Allan's autumn boulder. He pulled out his binoculars and focused on infinity. Drawing the glasses across the eastern horizon, he stopped when the lens was filled by a large Canadian flag. He had tied it to a poplar pole and lashed it to the chimney of the house.

He built a fire. Nestor had left his blankets on the woodpile. He draped one over his shoulders. Looking west, through a thickening sky, he recalled Nestor having said that in days past the area west of the river was considered the best hunting ground in the land. The old boys recognized it as being the last place on the planet they felt comfortable in because it hadn't yet been poisoned by industrialization.

It had taken him two long days to find three of the seventeen trees Grin had plotted on a crude map. The remaining fourteen, and hundreds more like them, would be felled with chainsaws, destined for a sawmill. They would be cut into planks and used for the construction of new houses in suburbia. They would become little else but wooden skeletons covered with gyprock and paint.

Grin had cut down one of the trees he had plotted on his tree map. Leonard could see the old boy, sweat dripping from his awkward old nose, pushing and pulling on a simple saw, bringing down a tree over a hundred years old. After having found three of the trees, he had a better understanding of how important they had been to Grin. He could better appreciate how they had represented a past when a free forest covered a free land.

He dug the raven out of the packsack and set it on a boulder. He stared into the fire and added more logs. Ragged flames chewed at the wood. He wondered if Watina could seem them.

Nestor had said Grin knew he was going to die. He wondered if Grin would have walked to the bridge to die alone or if Nestor would have taken him there for his last ride. Nestor had also said that once the timber berth was alive with the buzzing of fallers' saws it would be testament to the fact it would only be a matter of time before nothing was left of the free forest and the freedom it had represented to so many people. He wondered about a lot of things as the flames in front of him danced in the dying light.

55

He poked his head out of a soggy blanket. An inch of snow covered everything around him. Large snowflakes melted into his hair.

Countless images had raced through his mind as he lay beside a grey fire a million miles from sleep. He saw a young girl calling for help, her leg caught in a logjam. He saw Allan, lying broken in the ditch. Images of an elderly native man cutting down a tree thicker than the old man himself had filled his mind. While trying to roll a cigarette with trembling fingers he had thought about progress and how the old boys recognized it as being a term government and industry used at will to camouflage the devastation of the planet.

He gathered his belongings and limped to the bottom of the hill. Hobbling down the centre of the white road in front of him, he clutched Grin's bow saw in one hand, his walking stick in the other.

He was happy with the decision he had made beside a dying fire. He would make the acreage his new home. He would live on it and twist wrenches for Chap. He would learn about Kouetta.

He approached a bend in the road and tossed his walking stick aside. Leaning hard on the bow saw, he walked heavy on one side and vanished into the corner.